PRAISE FOR THE

LUMBERJANES

NOVELS

UNICORN POWER!

★ "Awesome to the max!"

—*Kirkus Reviews*, starred review

"Full o

"A hilarious and thoughtfully modern take on the classic
summer camp adventure that is destined to delight."

—*Shelf Awareness*

"A smart, silly, fast-paced adventure."

—*School Library Journal*

THE MOON IS UP

"More feisty feminist fun."

—*Kirkus Reviews*

LUMBERJANES

THE GOOD EGG

BOOK THREE

BY MARIKO TAMAKI
ILLUSTRATED BY BROOKLYN ALLEN

BASED ON THE LUMBERJANES COMICS
CREATED BY SHANNON WATTERS,
GRACE ELLIS, NOELLE STEVENSON & BROOKLYN ALLEN

AMULET BOOKS
NEW YORK

THE LIBRARY OF CONGRESS HAS CATALOGED
THE HARDCOVER EDITION AS FOLLOWS:

NAMES: TAMAKI, MARIKO, AUTHOR. | ALLEN, BROOKLYN A., ILLUSTRATOR.
TITLE: LUMBERJANES: THE GOOD EGG / BY MARIKO TAMAKI; ILLUSTRATED BY
BROOKLYN ALLEN.
DESCRIPTION: NEW YORK: AMULET BOOKS, 2018. | SERIES: LUMBERJANES; BOOK 3 |
BASED ON THE LUMBERJANES COMICS CREATED BY SHANNON WATTERS, GRACE ELLIS,
NOELLE STEVENSON & BROOKLYN ALLEN.
IDENTIFIERS: LCCN 2018017356 | ISBN 978-1-4197-3131-0 (HARDCOVER POB)
CLASSIFICATION: LCC PZ7.T1587 LUG 2018 | DDC [FIC]—DC23

PAPERBACK ISBN 978-1-4197-4092-3

PUBLISHED IN PAPERBACK IN 2020 BY AMULET BOOKS, AN IMPRINT OF ABRAMS.
ORIGINALLY PUBLISHED IN HARDCOVER BY AMULET BOOKS IN 2018. ALL RIGHTS
RESERVED. NO PORTION OF THIS BOOK MAY BE REPRODUCED, STORED IN A
RETRIEVAL SYSTEM, OR TRANSMITTED IN ANY FORM OR BY ANY MEANS, MECHANICAL,
ELECTRONIC, PHOTOCOPYING, RECORDING, OR OTHERWISE, WITHOUT WRITTEN
PERMISSION FROM THE PUBLISHER.

PRINTED AND BOUND IN U.S.A.
10 9 8 7 6 5 4 3 2 1

AMULET BOOKS ARE AVAILABLE AT SPECIAL DISCOUNTS WHEN PURCHASED IN
QUANTITY FOR PREMIUMS AND PROMOTIONS AS WELL AS FUNDRAISING OR
EDUCATIONAL USE. SPECIAL EDITIONS CAN ALSO BE CREATED TO SPECIFICATION.
FOR DETAILS, CONTACT SPECIALSALES@ABRAMSBOOKS.COM
OR THE ADDRESS BELOW.

AMULET BOOKS® IS A REGISTERED TRADEMARK OF
HARRY N. ABRAMS, INC.

ABRAMS The Art of Books
195 Broadway, New York, NY 10007
abramsbooks.com

FOR CHARLOTTE SHEEDY

—M.T.

LUMBERJANES

FIELD MANUAL

LUMBERJANES PLEDGE

I solemnly swear to do my best

Every day, and in all that I do,
To be brave and strong,

To be truthful and compassionate,

To be interesting and interested,

To pay attention and question
The world around me,

To think of others first,

To always help and protect my friends

~~To~~ ~~and~~ ~~faith~~ ~~in~~ ~~God~~

And to make the world a better place

For Lumberjane scouts
And for everyone else.

THEN THERE'S A LINE ABOUT GOD, OR WHATEVER

PART ONE

WILD THINGS
(I THINK I APPRECIATE YOU)

YOU'RE A STRANGE ANIMAL!

A Lumberjane should not only have the skills to survive in the wilderness (sometimes with limited resources) but also must appreciate the many creatures that call the wild outdoors their home.

The Wild Things badge requires scouts to learn how to track, observe, document, sketch, and record wild birds and animals in their natural habitats, to understand how creatures survive and thrive in the wild.

Scouts will learn how to coexist with wildlife, how to keep these animals safe and sound, and how to preserve as well as observe wild creatures.

Lumberjanes know that the wilderness has much to teach us. The more we understand about birds and animals, the more we understand . . .

CHAPTER 1

Famous researcher, scientist, and Lumberjane, Miss Jane Petunia Massy Acorn Dale once conducted an extensive study on the phenomenon of human grown-ups.

Jane wanted to understand what it was that made a grown-up a grown-up. To do this, she sought to observe grown-ups. To understand their ways and habits.

It was the only study she ever abandoned, because it was too annoying.

Grown-ups, she wrote in her extensive field notes, often declare that they are grown-up but cannot say why or when this happened. Even when questioned. Also, grown-ups are always quick to point out when someone is not a grown-up. Also, aside from clothing and cars, there is nothing particularly distinctive about grown-ups, compared to not-grown-ups. So they are bigger, Jane noted, so what?

In the end, the study yielded more questions and vague definitions than answers. So Jane went back to her research on birds and animals and felt much better about it.

The woods outside Miss Qiunzella Thiskwin Penniquiqul Thistle Crumpet's Camp for Hardcore Lady-Types have always been fruitful for the study of aviary and mammalian behavior.

On the morning that our story begins, the trees boomed with a cacophony of sounds.

A cacophony is kind of like a buffet of very different noises mixed together, but in a very awkward and loud way. So, really, it's more like how your plate looks after you visit a buffet, if it were possible to pile a plate high with SOUNDS.

In this case, sounds like:

SNNURT!

WHOO WHOO!

WEEEDY WEEEDY WEEEE

CHIT CHIT CCHHHIT

To name just a few.

Cacophonies, like buffets, aren't for everyone.

Some people like a lot of noise; the more noises together, the better.

Some people would just prefer if you would generally keep your voice down.

Lumberjanes tend to fall on the side of people who like noise, partly because noise is a big part of being a Lumberjane. There are cheers scouts like to cheer at dinner and campfire songs for campfire times. Also, there are many badges that specifically reward Lumberjanes for being loud, including: Let Your Trombone Slide, "Hear! Hear!" Give a Cheer, and, of course, the Yodeling badge, YODELA-HEEEWHOOO Wants to Know.

A scout with the WHOOO WHOOOO's Calling badge could have stood in the woods, closed their eyes, and caught the identifying features that make up the calls of wild boars, barn owls, flying squirrels, weasels, titmouses, and the fabulous blue-crested Ripley.

GEK-GGGEK

MURRROOOOOO

Tra la la!

The blue-crested Ripley, who will (you'll see) be the hero of this story, is a human creature and a Lumberjane with a shock of blue hair, a massive appetite, and a preference for orange clothing. Ripleys enjoy bouncing, running, jumping, frolicking, dancing, and singing, sometimes while sitting high up in very large pine trees, as she was on this particular morning.

LA LA LA!

Singing is how Ripleys keep track of things and goings-on and whatnot. Because Ripleys, unlike Aprils or Jos, are not really into writing things down in notebooks and journals.

This, of course, is fine. Because everyone, every creature, is different.

Some scouts like to write things down. Some, like Ripley's very good friend and fellow Roanoke cabin member April, like to write and underline things and draw a picture and write more notes and then highlight the whole thing with a bright yellow highlighter.

Some don't.

For Ripley, writing things down was a very slow process that was very unlike bouncing.

Which Ripley much preferred.

Singing is a little like bouncing. Especially if the song comes from that bouncy castle in your heart.

On this day, Ripley was singing about a mouse named Castor, who was also a Moon Pirate and whose Lumberjane story had come to a close recently, when she climbed back into her space pirate ship and soared up into the sky.

THE GOOD EGG

Castor loves cheese, Ripley sang.
And glitter if you please
She lives on a ship
She's taking a trip
To the moooooooon
What else is happening?
Well let's see
Lots of things hap-pen to me
So, also I have found . . .

Ripley flipped her legs up and tipped backward, swinging around and grabbing onto the branch. Still holding on with one hand, she dangled down over . . .

. . . a big nest
Of really really really really big golden eggs

Of course, when describing something as big or little, it is worth noting that "big" and "little" are subjective terms, which is to say, one person's notion of BIG could be relatively small compared to someone else's. This is most often noted when cake is being served.

Still, most people would have to admit that the nest below Ripley was HUGE. It was as big as a cabin. The eggs, most of the eggs, were as big as Ripley. With one exception.

THE GOOD EGG

And a little gold egg that I like best.

Eggie was a smaller, basketball-size egg that Ripley had noticed on the edge of the nest.

"Hello, Eggie," Ripley trilled happily.

A basketball-size egg would probably be considered a big egg if you put it next to the kind of eggs you normally find in nests. If you put it next to a robin's egg—which are so small you can fit three in your hand, depending on how big your hand is—the basketball-size egg would be . . . enormous.

But in its nest surrounded by its massive siblings, Eggie was tiny.

Wee even.

Ripley dropped down from her branch and leaned in close to the nest.

"How are you today, Eggie? Are you egg-cellent?"

Eggs, generally, do not make noise. Yet. They are PRE-noise. So Eggie said nothing. But Ripley liked to say encouraging things to it all the same.

"Anyway," Ripley said, smiling at Eggie, "it was really nice hanging out with you. I gotta go, but I'll see you tomorrow, okay?"

Eggie sat silent.

"Kay, see ya!"

Ripley skipped off to camp, her feet crunching into the forest floor with every step. It was time to go do scout things. The day, and the story of Ripley, was just beginning, and there was much to do.

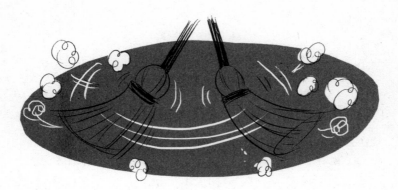

CHAPTER 2

A happy camp is, among other things, a clean and orderly camp.

Mostly because it's just really annoying to step on something, like a whiffle bat or a rake, when you're not expecting to step on something.

Also, keeping things orderly makes it easier to finish jigsaw puzzles.

As former head counselor Mademoiselle Suzannah Saror Mareng Salamader III once noted, "Everything has a place, and so everything in its place, and if it's not there, that's minus two points."

This was, of course, back when there was a points system.

Which there isn't, anymore.

Currently, the philosophy of Miss Qiunzella Thiskwin Penniquiqul Thistle Crumpet's Camp for Hardcore Lady-Types was: Cleanliness is next to awesomeness.

As part of the GREAT CABIN CLEANUP, the scouts of Roanoke cabin—actually the whole camp, including Dartmoor, Woolpit, Zodiac, Roswell, Dighton, and even Aurora—were cabin cleaning.

Jen, the counselor for Roanoke cabin, stood on the steps in her recently ironed green and yellow uniform with matching clipboard, a newly polished whistle dangling around her neck. Her eyes shone with excitement, and her beret was perfectly angled on the top of her head for maximum beret effect. Jen liked putting things in order.

Cleaning was something Jen enjoyed almost as much as Ripley enjoyed singing or bouncing.

"ALL RIGHT, SCOUTS!" Jen shouted as she marched down the stairs. "I WANT TO SEE ALL THE CLUTTER, ALL THE STUFF, EVERYTHING UNDER YOUR BUNKS, OVER YOUR BUNKS, BETWEEN YOUR BUNKS, ALL THE MESS, CLEANED UP! LET'S GO! LET'S DO THIS!"

April emerged from Roanoke carrying a pile of stuff almost as big as April was, which is about four and a half feet high (and all muscle).

ALL MUSCLE!

"How did we get so much stuff?" April grumbled, plonking the pile on the grass outside the cabin and brushing off her purple jacket, which was currently more dust gray than plum purple.

April didn't mind cleaning so much as she thought there were a million other things—getting badges, climbing mountains, solving mysteries—that they, Roanoke cabin, could be doing INSTEAD of cleaning.

What is cleaning if not looking at a bunch of stuff you already know about? she thought.

A puff of dust, like a giant cough, plumed out of Roanoke cabin's door, followed by Molly, who was rolling a boulder of stuff down the stairs. Molly's boulder looked like a meteor that had traveled extensively through space and collected, on its path, a mix of cosmic debris, all while hurtling toward the earth.

Actually, it was stuff that Molly and Bubbles, Molly's raccoon and hat, had just pulled out from under Molly's bunk. With great combined effort.

At home, Molly had to do a cleanup every day, so once in a blue moon didn't seem too bad. Also, Molly was not one to grumble, generally.

Molly was more of a blusher than a grumbler. And when Molly blushed, her whole face went the color of a tomato. Which was really embarrassing.

Molly's mystery meteor bounced down the stairs and onto the grass, where it collapsed in a heap next to April's pile with a soft *PFFFT* sound. Almost like it had given up on the idea of being a meteor, right at that moment.

"What the literal junk!" April exclaimed, looking at Molly.

"The weird thing is, I don't even recognize this junk," Molly said, holding her hands up near her face in a "Geez, I don't know" gesture. Molly's green baseball tee was also covered in dust. "I think maybe some of this is Bubbles's."

Bubbles the raccoon, who was so covered in dust he looked like a gray cat, blinked innocently, reached surreptitiously (which means in a way that is trying to avoid notice) into the wad, pulled out a pawful of nuts, and scampered back into the cabin to deposit them under Molly's bed.

Minutes later, Jo emerged from the cabin with her cleanup items: a small pile of folded notes that she had discovered tucked into one of the books next to her bed and two tiny silver screws she had found under her pillow.

"Wait." April shook her head in disbelief. "Is THAT all your junk?"

Jo didn't like to think of anything as junk, since Jo knew just about everything had a possible use.

"This is my recycling," she noted, neatly sliding her pile of papers into the recycling bin and pocketing the screws in one of her many pockets.

Beyond reusing whatever could be reused, Jo also liked to keep things tidy. At home, in her science lab, everything was neatly labeled and ordered. Because science is

13

also generally neat and ordered. Even if the things you're researching . . . aren't.

Ripley liked to think of herself as sort of a tidy person.

Ripley liked to keep her clothes on the floor, but this did not mean Ripley was not a tidy person. A person can be a person who leaves their shirt on the floor so it is easier to slip into said shirt in the morning and still be a tidy person. Ripley's sister, who shared a room with her at home, disagreed.

Mostly what Ripley found when she went spelunking under her bunk was lots of glitter, which seemed to have rained down from her mattress and formed a thin layer of sparkle on the floor.

Which then got all over Ripley.

So Ripley's cleanup was walking outside covered in glitter and bouncing up and down until all the glitter came off, forming a sort of shimmery halo around her. Like a rainbow, only better.

"Aw," Molly said, looking over. "You're so sparkly! Where's your garbage?"

"Don't have any!" Ripley chirped.

"Keep cleaning!" Jen called over as she marched between cabins. "All library books should go back to the library! All odds and ends should go to the craft pile. All garbage goes in a landfill, so think very carefully before you put it in the garbage. Recycle! Reuse! CLEAN!"

"How come I have so much stuff?" April asked no one in particular, putting one foot on her pile. "This is a truly Sisyphean task, my friends."

The classic Sisyphean task involved rolling a rock up a hill, watching the rock roll down the hill, and then rolling it back up again. Not exactly like cleaning a cabin, but both can feel kind of endless.

The pile under April's foot burbled and slowly began sucking in her shoe.

"AUGH!" April jumped back. "The pile! The pile has a mind of its own!!"

"Hey," Ripley said, dusting glitter off her hands, "so I was visiting my eggs today."

"Your aunts?" Jo asked, looking closely at one of the screws from her pocket and trying to decide where, exactly, it had come from.

"Eggs," Ripley repeated.

"Hey, look, you guys!" Mal stepped out of the cabin with what looked like, and was, a massive tumbleweed. "I looked under my bunk and I found . . . socks!"

"It's a Lumberjane miracle," Jo said.

"Are they YOUR socks?" Molly asked.

"Geez." Mal dropped the pile on the grass. "It's been so long since I've seen them, I don't even know."

Mal bent over and shook the dust out of her short black hair and off the many buttons on her vest.

At home, Mal's room was sometimes so messy she could roll out of bed and onto the floor and not even know it.

"A nest full of eggs," Ripley said, turning to April, who was now elbow deep in her pile.

"Hey!" April yanked her hand out of her pile and held up a tattered paperback. "Check it! It's my copy of *Tales from the Mermaid City*!"

It was an issue of the Mermaid Lemonade Stand series April had already read, many times, but it was a good one.

"Did you say Annette?" Molly looked up from rummaging through her pile, which WAS, it turns out, mostly acorns that Bubbles had been stowing under her bed. A cloud of dust hovered around Molly's head like a little private storm cloud. "Who's Annette?"

"A nest," Ripley said, again. Repeating herself. Again.

Molly stuck her finger in her ear and shook her head. "My ears are full of dust, you guys."

Ripley frowned.

Sometimes when you are smaller, the things you say are just not as big as the rest of the stuff going on.

Or at least this is how it seems when you are Ripley-size or a Ripley-like person.

Ripley was used to this as someone who got ready for school every morning in a house full of brothers and sisters who were older and louder than she was.

"What, sweetie?" was sort of Ripley's second name at home.

It was okay, but it was still kind of annoying.

Molly smiled, bending down to look at Ripley's frowning glittery face. "A nest sounds cooler than Annette," she said.

Ripley nodded. And opened her mouth to say more, but then, as often happens at a place where lots of stuff is happening all the time, there was a sudden clanging.

"CAMPERS! TIDY UP AND MEET AT THE MESS HALL FOR A BIG ANNOUNCEMENT!" Jen bellowed into her shiny megaphone.

"Tell me about it later," Molly whispered.

Ripley nodded, her face still glittery, especially on the bridge of her nose.

"Oooooooh. A big announcement." April whistled, abandoning her mysterious pile for a new adventure. "SOUNDS BIG!"

"Big relative to what?" Jo asked, striding with her big strides to the mess hall.

"BIG!" Ripley danced past them in a fog of leftover iridescence. "Let's go!"

CHAPTER 3

With a general buzz of excitement crackling in the air, the Lumberjanes gathered in the dining hall for a very big announcement.

Sitting with her cabin, Ripley wondered if the big announcement would mean getting another visitor, like how Castor the space mouse had showed up the last time they had the big Galaxy Wars announcement.

Ripley wondered if making big announcements made other things happen at camp. Like pulling a magic lever.

Ripley was not wrong. One big thing did seem to lead to another at Miss Qiunzella Thiskwin Penniquiqul Thistle Crumpet's Camp for Hardcore Lady-Types.

April wondered if the big announcement was that there was going to be another prize that they could win. "Maybe it's a CUP." She gasped, clapping her hands together. "Or a TROPHY!"

"I don't know," Jo said. "We just cleaned out our cabin. Do we really want a prize? Prizes take up a lot of space."

April drummed her fingers together. "There's ALWAYS room for prizes."

"Like pancakes," Ripley said, knowingly.

The buzz in the mess hall was growing. Every second was buzzier and buzzier, like when you're walking and you get close to an actual nest of bees.

Which is what you have to do if you're looking to get your BEE-HAVE badge. But it's not otherwise recommended.

"LISTEN UP!" Vanessa—Zodiac counselor, her hair currently slicked into two prominent purple spikes, which some people (including Vanessa) thought made her look tough—stood at the front of the hall. She waved for quiet; the buzz continued.

"I SAID, LISTEN UP!" Vanessa barked, her spikes stiff and unmoving as she spoke.

A relative silence rippled over the crowd.

"My fellow camp counselors and I have decreed that, post Galaxy Wars, which was a very successful and educational but exhausting cabin versus cabin spectacular, we need to do a camp-wide activity that brings us back to the true meaning of being a Lumberjane, which is . . ."

"FRIENDSHIP TO THE MAX!" Ripley boomed with great feeling, because it was really important.

"Exactly!" Vanessa pointed at Ripley. "Also, we thought maybe we'd do something that involved less . . . planning."

Vanessa looked at Jen. Jen looked back at Vanessa with the look of someone who thinks giving up sleeping and eating to get something done, and done well, is no big deal.

Jen had also spent the first three days after Galaxy Wars in bed sleeping, which was fascinating to Ripley, who had never seen someone sleep that long.

Also, Jen sang in her sleep.

Mostly eighties power ballads and a little of what sounded like nineties rap hits.

"What the TLC?" April had exclaimed on the second day (and fortieth hour) of sleep. "Is she still singing?"

It was after this extensive slumber that Jen and the rest of the counselors had a long meeting about the general state of camp. It was here Vanessa brought up the idea that it would be nice for the campers to do something a little less competitive and more cooperative.

Friendship to the Max, after all, doesn't mean "except for other cabins."

Also, Vanessa had pointed out, maybe they could do something a little more chill.

"I'm into this," Molly said. "We could use a little more co-cabin cooperation."

"We already play music with Wren," Mal noted. "And I'm on a whiffle ball team with half of Dighton."

"The very competitive half," Jo noted. "I'm surprised they're even here and not practicing."

"I tap dance with Barney," Ripley added. "And Bubbles."

"Barney can tap dance now too?" Jo looked impressed. "That's cool."

"Okay." Jen waved her hands. "Settle down, scouts! So. In that spirit, this next activity will not be a competition. It *will* involve you working in groups of mixed cabins. This project was specifically designed to teach you new skills AND promote your efforts to improve teamwork and productivity.

"Yes. And so . . ." Jen paused. "Uh, without further ado. To, uh, announce your next activity. I'm pleased to introduce . . . uh HAHAHAHAHAA."

Jen put a finger against her lips. "Sorry about that. Just a little. Giggle. Um. Vanessa, would you tee-hee take over?"

Vanessa stepped forward. And leaned into Jen. "What is wrong with you?"

Jen shook her head.

Vanessa squinted. "Are you okay?"

"Just announce AnnaHAHAHA. AnnaHAHAHAHA." Jen clamped her hand over her mouth.

"Our guest," she mumbled through her fingers.

"Uh, okay." Vanessa looked around. "Speaking of which, where is she? She said she wanted to make an entrance . . ."

"What's wrong with Jen?" Molly whispered, craning to see over the heads of the other scouts.

"Maybe she just thought of a really good joke?" Mal wondered.

Up at the front of the mess hall, Vanessa threw her hands into the air. "Well, she can't make an entrance if she's not here," she hissed.

Jen nodded, fingers still firmly clamped over her mouth.

Vanessa raised an eyebrow. "Seriously, what is going on with you?"

"Th-heehhee-ater," Jen managed. "It makes me—"

Suddenly, the hall . . . went . . . black.

"Who turned out the lights?!"

Music ripped through the hall.

DUN DUN DUN DUUUUUUUUN!

Jen reached for her flashlight. Mal gripped Molly's hand and Molly gripped Mal's.

Bubbles jumped off of Molly's head and grabbed onto Ripley's face like it was a life raft. Ripley wrapped her arms around Bubbles and turned her head to the side so she could breathe.

April jumped up on the bench and assumed a wide defensive position. Which is standing in a way that you could karate kick someone in the face no matter which way they come at you.

It takes some balance to stand this way.

Jo waited for the lights to come back on.

DUN DUN DUN DUUUUUUUUUN!

THUNK!

A spotlight appeared at the front of the hall, forming a circle of potent white light into which stepped, or rather, glided, the one and only resident drama instructor, Miss Annabella Panache.

Miss Annabella Panache was the most like a movie star of anyone Ripley had ever seen sort of up close.

Standing in the spotlight, her hands up, fingers stiff in gesture, Miss Annabella Panache tilted her chin up into the light. Batted her long lashes. Took a deep breath. Held her pose a moment longer.

23

The rest of the room . . . stopped . . . breathing.

Just for a second.

"I told you I wanted to make a DRAMATIC entrance," she said, her voice resonant and bold. "YES! And so I HAVE."

"HOLY SPLIT BRITCHES," April gasped, her hands on both cheeks, her eyes sparkling with excitement. "WE'RE MAKING A PLAY!"

"JUSTIN VIVIAN BOND." Jo grinned. "I think you're right."

CHAPTER 4

April WAS right.

Generally, Annabella Panache preferred a stage, but as a professional, she could make do with any space she was given, and tonight it was the mess hall.

Annabella looked out into her audience of attentive scouts and stretched out her arms, palms up, like an opera singer getting ready for a big note.

Everyone was spellbound. Even Bubbles stopped chirping and clung to Ripley's neck, waiting to see what Panache would do next.

"THEATER," she boomed, using three syllables instead of two. "WHAT IS THE-AH-TAH?"

April shot her hand into the air and then lowered it quietly when she realized this was a speech, not a question.

The spotlight followed Miss Panache as she waltzed from table to table.

"Theater is IMAGINATION. Theater is STORYTELL-ING. Theater is COMMUNITY. Theater is ART. Yes."

When she said YES, Panache pulled her hands toward her and tightened them into fists.

Then, BOOM, in a flash, she tossed her hands over her head, her golden nails shimmering in the light.

"Theater is LIFE!! YES!"

Ripley managed to peel Bubbles away from her face so she could look up at the towering figure that was Miss Panache.

Panache's big gold hair reminded Ripley of her eggs.

Miss Panache's hair was about as big as Eggie. Which is big, for hair. Also, her hair smelled like chemicals and roses. When Miss Panache moved, her hair stayed stiff and still, like Vanessa's spikes.

"On this day, we set a course for SELF-EXPRESSION!" she cried. "As you and your fellow scouts, you and your fellow THESPIANS, will combine forces to create works. VISIONS. MANIFESTATIONS. MANIFESTOS?"

"A thespian," April whispered into Ripley's ear, "is an actor."

"Oh." Ripley nodded.

"So how do we begin this journey to creative, to NEW, to UNBOUNDED WORLDS? Yes. To begin. Each group has been assigned a classic tale." Miss Panache moved to the front of the room, where Jen and Vanessa had set up a series of cards tacked to the wall.

"These tales you and your fellow theater creators will INTERPRET for the modern day and PRESENT for your peers using a particular focus on either movement or . . ."

Miss Panache twirled her fingers as she thought. ". . . musicality, or dramatic effect. What have you."

"Is it a competition?" April asked under her breath.

"This will be AN EVENT!" Miss Panache roared. "It is a chance to share your passions and your gifts with your fellow scouts. It is a chance to MOVE and BE MOVED."

"I don't think it's a competition," Jo whispered.

Ripley noticed that Miss Panache's eyebrows were so high, they disappeared when she said big things.

Like, EVENT!

Also, when Miss Panache said things, it looked like a shock of energy was running through her whole body. Like a little piece of lightning.

"Now." Miss Panache glided to the front of the room, like she was riding a tiny cloud. "What stories will you be telling? Yes. That is the question, and the answer is . . ."

The spotlight hit the cards, illuminating the tales that each group would perform.

"First! Sleeping SCOUT," she began, "a retelling of the story of a woman betrayed by society and family who finds support in a new community, only to have her fortune affected by outside forces!"

"Is that Sleeping Beauty?" Mal whispered.

"It's a RETELLING of Sleeping Beauty," Molly said, tilting her head to the side. "I think."

"Yes," Mal said.

"Scouts in this troupe will employ the art of Butoh, a challenging but majestic form of movement that emphasizes the element of TIME."

"Cool," Jo said.

"Scout-erella! A glass slipper. A fairy godmother fixated on societal norms of success. Cruelty. Justice. A story told in tap, step, and modern dance! YES!"

In the back of the room, Barney, sitting with Zodiac cabin, crossed their fingers.

"The Scout who cried WOLF! An opera! A vocalization, possibly a rumination on the role of modern media!"

"This feels a little complicated," Vanessa murmured.

Jen was afraid to open her mouth and so just silently agreed that this was somewhat over-the-top.

Which, actually, is pretty Lumberjane, so, okay.

28

"The SCOUT and the BEAST! A musical for the instrumentalists. A love story? YES."

Mal beamed and poked Molly's side.

"And finally, a dramatic take on the classic family epic GOLDI-SCOUT AND THE THREE BEARS! Forces colliding, interacting, interpreting each other? YES!"

Vanessa stepped into the spotlight.

"Your very thoughtful counselors have taken the time to put you into groups," she said. "We've mixed up cabins so you'll have a chance to collaborate with different scouts."

The scouts hummed with excitement, poised to dash to the front of the room.

"Okay," Vanessa said, stepping forward. "Go ahead and take a look."

The room was suddenly awash in thundering scouts clamoring to the front to see which play they were doing.

Mal and Molly were placed in the musical group, much to Mal and Molly's delight.

April, Jo, and Ripley were teamed up with Wren and Hes from Zodiac to tell the story of Goldi-Scout and the Three Bears.

"Consider these STORIES as opportunities," Miss Panache called into the crowd. "To TELL. To REtell these stories."

Emphasis on RE.

YES.

Humming with excitement, the scouts assembled into their groups and headed to the picnic tables in front of the mess hall to get to work.

Several minutes later, Ripley sat at a table next to the flagpole with her group and watched April light up with ideas, as Hes and Wren, from Zodiac cabin, observed, seemingly cautiously optimistic, or just cautious.

"You guys!" April cheered the way a person who is used to pumping up the energy in the room like a balloon cheers. "This is going to be AWESOME!"

"Okay," Hes said, guardedly.

"Sure." Wren shrugged.

Ripley nodded. Although really, Ripley, who liked PLAY-ING more than plays, was wondering how Eggie was doing.

Egg Egg
How are you?
If you were a Robin's Egg
You'd be blue
I wish I was there with you
Egg Egg
How are you?

CHAPTER 5

Later that evening, at dinner, Rosie sat at her usual table in the mess hall and took a moment of respite from the day's very vigorous activities.

A respite is a mini-vacation for people who are very bad at taking vacations, which Lumberjanes generally are.

Because Lumberjanes, generally, would rather go discover something than get a tan by the pool.

Generally, for Rosie, a respite was just long enough for a cup of very refreshing nettle tea.

Around her, Lumberjanes chowed down on Kzyzzy's infamous Vegan No Clam, No Ma'am Chowder, making the usual amount of noise for Lumberjanes at dinner.

Which is a lot of noise.

Rosie stretched out in her chair, accidentally dislodging a clump of mud from her caked hiking boots.

"Hello, Rosie." Jen appeared next to her table, a smile on her face, which, if you knew Jen, was a nervous smile, partly because Rosie, while being amazing, was also intimidating.

As many amazing people are.

And partly because Jen was afraid of what was going to happen when she opened her mouth.

"Joyce!" Rosie trumpeted, raising a glass of nettle tea. "How did it go today?"

"Well, it's Jen," Jen said, her back stiffening. "And I think it went very well. Miss AnnaHHAHAAHA. Ahem. Miss AnnaHAHAHA."

"Miss Annabella Panache," Rosie offered, with an eyebrow raise.

Jen nodded. "Was great."

"Are you all right?" Rosie raised an eyebrow. "You seem very . . . giggly."

"Fine." Jen coughed. "Ahem. Apologies. *She* seems very t-talented. And . . . inventive?"

"She is a star of stage and screen, Josephine," Rosie said, taking a sip of soothing tea. "We are lucky to have her. So, the scouts will all be performing plays?"

"Yes." Jen nodded. "We divided them up with a mix of

different scouts from each cabin, as I, *Jen*, suggested. We also have workshops set up for various other—"

Jen paused. Composed herself. "Thee-hee-hee-atrical skills."

"Theatrical skills," Rosie repeated, careful to enunciate. "Yes, indeed. Are you a fan of the theatrical arts yourself, Jin?"

Jen sighed. "It's complicated."

"It's complicated" is something people say sometimes when it seems even more complicated to say the actual reason for something. Something, like, say, crippling stage fright that triggers an intense giggling reaction in response to the very mention of . . .

Theater.

Also: stage, acting, drama.

Also: Annabella Panache.

"Well, then." Rosie stood up, downed the last bit of nettley goodness, and stepped toward the door. "Should be quite an exciting week!"

Jen, and it was JEN, hugged her clipboard to her chest and sighed.

Meanwhile, at Roanoke cabin's table, April was trying to figure out who Miss Annabella Panache looked like. April thought she looked like the Mermaid Professor from the Mermaid Lemonade Stand mystery *Sea Average: A Mermaid Educational Adventure.*

Most of the rest of Roanoke, indeed most of the rest of the population, had never heard of that book. Although it is a pretty good book.

Mal held her hands out next to her face. "I love her hair and how it wings away from her face and then just keeps winging."

"And it smells like roses," Ripley said.

"Pretty sure that's a bucket of hair spray," Mal added, reverently. "Maximum hold."

"I like when she goes like this," April said, making her eyes wide and leaning back, looking like a cat that just saw a dancing photocopier. "I think that would be good to put in our play, that move."

"I'm sure we'll be doing lots of moves," Jo said, although, honestly, making a play was less interesting to Jo than making a THING.

"It's not MOVES, it's MOVEMENT," April said, a knowing finger raised. "Or something. Anyway, our play is going to be the best play EVER. Right, Rip?"

Ripley nodded, her mouth full of a very large spoonful of chowder.

"Oh." April grinned, turning to Mal and Molly. "Except for yours. Maybe it will only be a little better than yours."

Mal smiled. "Art is subjective," she noted. "But ours is going to rock. Malka already figured out the instrumentation. We're going to do a series of love songs that deconstruct standards of beauty, replacing references to beauty with references to intelligence."

"Holy Barbra Streisand," April gasped. "That's a really good idea."

"YES." Mal grinned. "Plus, our group is so cool. Maggie May plays the tuba. Marcy plays the triangle. Malka plays the drums. I play guitar and sing, and Molly plays the accordion.

"And maybe," Mal said, elbowing Molly playfully, "Molly will sing."

Molly blushed. "Maybe."

"You guys figured all that out." April frowned. "We still haven't figured out staging! Or casting! Or anything!"

"Well, what did you spend all afternoon talking about?" Mal asked.

"THE-A-TER!" April gasped, holding her hands up like Miss Panache.

April dropped her hands. "Patty Jenkins, we're behind."

Ripley picked up her bowl. "I need more chowder," she said.

Ripley didn't think April needed her to figure out how to make the best play ever.

Figuring out that stuff was something April did all the time.

At the counter, waiting in line, Ripley bumped into Barney, who met her with a big Barney grin.

"Hey, Rip!" Barney chirped. "What play are you doing?"

"Three bears." Ripley shrugged. "You?"

"Sleeping Scout," Barney said. "I was hoping I would get to be SCOUT-ERELLA, but I guess people think I'm more Butoh than tap? Anyhoo. It's no big deal."

Barney gave a little shrug that almost made them drop the book tucked under their arm. Which was easy to do because it was a really big book.

Ripley pointed. "What are you reading?"

"Oh!" Barney's eyes lit up. "It's for my next badge! Hatch You Later! Which I am taking in conjunction with my Animal Habitat-ery badge. Which I am taking in conjunction with my Hello Birdie badge for bird watching."

All these conjunctions meant Barney was doing a lot of things at once. Which was the Barney way.

Ripley was so excited, she almost dropped her chowder. "WHAT? That's so cool! I found a nest! A really big nest! And it's really big! And the eggs are GOLD!"

Barney was so excited, they almost dropped their chowder. "GOLD EGGS? That's amazing! Where is it?"

"In the woods." Ripley was bouncing with enthusiasm.

Barney bit their lip. "This could be an incredible opportunity to practice my ODD skills! Could you take me there? Tomorrow morning?"

"Are you kidding?" Ripley squealed. "That would be awesome!"

"I'll meet you at the edge of the tree line," Barney said. "At sunrise."

Ripley nodded vigorously. "Yep yep!"

Back at Roanoke's table, April had pulled out her notebook and was furiously scribbling.

"Okay," she said, mostly to herself, "we just need to be more organized. I'll come up with a chart of basic concepts and genres. And then I can write—"

"Or *we* could write," Jo said, tapping April's notebook gently with her spoon.

"Right, right." April bit her pencil, then continued scribbling. "Holy Lisa Kron, this is going to be great!"

"Yes," Jo said.

Spinning her spoon on the table, Ripley smiled. "Barney and I are going back to see the eggs again tomorrow."

Everyone at the table was talking, all at once, a cacophony of noise that swallowed up Ripley's little voice.

"What did you say?" Molly asked, turning to Ripley. "Sorry, we were talking about tubas."

"It's okay." Ripley smiled, digging into her soup. "Tubas are cool."

For the rest of the meal, as Ripley polished off her third bowl of chowder and April wrote in her notebook, a song rattled through Ripley's brain.

THE GOOD EGG

Eggs eggs eggs eggs
Short eggs
Tall eggs
Summer winter fall eggs
Big eggs
Small eggs
First eggs
Third eggs
Very very
Very big bird eggs
Eggs eggs eggs eggs.

CHAPTER 6

The next morning, in the crisp light of early sunrise, Barney stood waiting for Ripley at the edge of the woods, in their cap and newly ironed uniform.

"Hey, you still have glitter on you," they said when Ripley appeared. Ripley was looking slightly wrinkled and sleepy and, yes, still coated in glitter but very excited.

"It twinkles in the morning light." Ripley grinned, pointing to the sparkles still stuck to her sweatshirt as they headed into the woods.

"I got so excited after we talked," Barney admitted, stepping carefully over the loose branches on the ground. "I was up until midnight looking at books in the library. I looked at some of Miss Jane Petunia Massy Acorn Dale's old notes from some of her original texts, which are just . . ." Barney sighed, "truly fabulous specimens of ODD methodology."

"Yeah," Ripley said. "Um. I meant to ask you what that is . . . the ODD thing?"

Sometimes Ripley didn't like asking people what stuff was because it seemed to make people think Ripley didn't know stuff (which she did). But Barney was a good person to ask questions because Barney was one of the few people that Ripley had ever met who actually liked to explain things. It made them happy. Also, Barney didn't ever assume Ripley didn't know something.

"That's a great question." Barney smiled. "ODD is the process, that is, the methodology or method, of scientific analysis, which is a way of looking at things in a scientific way. This specific way was invented and innovated by Miss Jane Petunia Massy Acorn Dale. ODD is an acronym for Observe, Document, and DO NOT TOUCH. Yes?"

Miss Jane Petunia Massy Acorn Dale—stamp collector, jump roper, figure skater, groundbreaking gluten-free baker, and esteemed biologist—was also, actually, gloriously odd in the regular way as well, but Barney had never met her and so did not know this.

Jane was also, just as an aside, the former reigning champion of most (gluten-free) pancakes eaten in one sitting, before Ripley.

"The ODD approach," Barney said, with great pride, "is what we're going to use to research this nest!"

"Amazing! Did Miss Jane Petunia Massy Acorn Dale ever write about any gold eggs?" Ripley asked, bouncing.

Barney shook their head. "She did not. But she did see plenty of large birds. She was even the first person to spot a Wawa Bird, which is twice as big as an ostrich and very silly.

"I was thinking about what you said, though," Barney noted, "about the eggs you found being really really big. And it made me think of our first Lumberjane adventure together, which also involved a big bird, a very very big bird, which got me thinking . . ."

"Yup yup." Ripley nodded. "Thinking is awesome."

"I was thinking," Barney continued, "that the eggs you describe could be from a creature that is not necessarily something you would find in the pages of a regular biology book."

"Oooooooh." Ripley hopped over a tree trunk. "That would be super cool."

"I mean," Barney said, pushing their black hair out of their face as they strolled through the woods, "I get the impression a Lumberjane can NEVER rule that sort of thing out, since I am staying in a cabin that is the cabin of a Greek god."

"Where *is* Diane?" Ripley asked, twirling.

"Family reunion."

Suddenly, Ripley had an amazing idea. "MARY BLAIR! DO YOU THINK THE EGG IS A UNICORN EGG?!"

"Hmmmm," Barney considered. "Although there are some creatures other than birds, like turtles, that lay eggs, there aren't a lot of equine creatures that lay eggs. That I know of."

"Jumpin' Judy Garland, this is exciting," Ripley cheered.

The two picked up speed, weaving through the trees as birds took flight and scattered out of their way.

As they closed in on the nest, Ripley's mouth popped open. "OH MY GOSH!"

"OH, HEY!" Barney said. "They hatched!"

CHAPTER 7

The nest was full of massive shards of broken shells, scattered throughout the nest like the remnants of a raucous tea party.

"Aw," Ripley said, her hands on her cheeks. "I mean . . . yay."

It wasn't that Ripley didn't want the eggs to hatch. Obviously, she did. That's what eggs do, after all.

Ripley's mom once told her that every person is an egg who will one day hatch and go on to become whatever it is they were meant to be.

Still, it's sad when hatching means that something you liked, like an egg called Eggie, is gone.

Barney stood back and pulled a notebook out of their back pocket. "This," they said, "this is a truly incredible discovery, Ripley. Even with the eggs hatched, this is an amazing opportunity to employ the ODD approach and learn more about what creatures made and laid eggs in this nest."

"Okay." Ripley turned to Barney. "What do we do first?"

"First," Barney said, pointing at the nest, "we OBSERVE whatever creature or natural wonder we have come upon."

"So, the nest?" Ripley sounded a little unsure.

"Yes." Barney pulled out their notebook. "Second step, we DOCUMENT by taking down notes, sketching, or photographing the phenomenon or habitat or creature in question."

Ripley nodded. "Oh-kay!"

"And finally," Barney noted, hovering over the nest, careful not to touch it with their kerchief, "and most importantly, we DO NOT (no matter what else we do) DISTURB whatever it is we are looking at."

Ripley took a careful step back from the nest. "Right. That's good. Don't do that. Got it."

"This is especially crucial when it comes to nests and burrows," Barney explained, "because a nest is a home. And a good researcher, as much and however possible, respects the integrity of all creatures."

Ripley nodded vigorously. Ripley knew that you don't just go bouncing around someone else's home, even if they're not there.

Not if you're a proper Lumberjane.

"Yes!" Ripley cheered. "Holy Jane Goodall, this is soooooo cool!"

Barney stood, looking.

It looked like Barney had become a Barney statue.

"Um." Ripley shoved her hands into her pockets. "So, what are we doing?"

"We're observing." Barney stepped closer to the nest, careful not to touch the sides.

"Oh," Ripley said. She hadn't realized this observing thing took so long.

She turned to look at the nest.

And looked at the nest.

Nest, she thought. This is. A nest.

Ripley looked back at Barney.

Barney seemed to still be hard at work, observing. In a way that Ripley was not.

Ripley grabbed onto her elbow and pushed her toe into the soft dirt around the nest. "Uh. Barney?"

"Yes?" Barney looked up, bright-eyed.

"What's an observation?" she asked. "Because, I think maybe I'm just looking . . . at the nest."

"That's another great question!" Barney smiled. "Ripley,

you have such great questions! Actually, they're very similar. Looking is seeing with your eyes, and observing is looking and then using what you see to understand something about what you're seeing. So really, observing is like looking, but more carefully. It's looking at details."

Barney stepped in front of the nest and pointed at it with their pencil.

"So, for example, there are a lot of details about this nest we can observe. Like, it's really big. In this case, roughly twenty feet in diameter," they noted. "Another detail is that it appears to be made of mostly local flora and tree branches, including pine and oak."

"Now"—Barney stood up on their tiptoes—"let's look inside the nest. Do you remember how many eggs there were?"

Ripley closed her eyes and tried to flip the pages of her brain back to the day before. "Five," she said. "Four big eggs and Li'l Eggie."

"Eggie?"

"The big eggs were all big like me," Ripley explained. "But Eggie was smaller, like half as big."

"Now that"—Barney winked—"is some eggspertise."

Ripley grinned. Puns always made Ripley think of April, the pun master.

Barney stepped up on a rock to get a closer look inside the nest. Ripley did the same.

"What do you notice about the shells?" Barney asked.

"They're cracked. And they look like pizza pieces," Ripley said. "They're gold and shiny, but . . . inside the shell they look silver."

Barney nodded, quickly jotting all the details into their notebook. "Anything else?"

Ripley hopped off the rock and started walking around the nest.

"Feathers," she said. "Soft-looking feathers."

The nest was now full of downy fluff, fine fluffy feathery snowflakes ranging in color from ivory to a soft pink, she noted.

"Plus some very big feathers," Barney added, pointing to a single, long, golden feather sticking up out of the center of the nest like a sail. "Which could mean, but may not mean, a big bird."

Ripley took another few steps around the nest. Looking and observing.

"OH, LOOK!" she cried. "A hole!"

"A what?" Barney looked up from their sketch of several of the larger pieces of shell.

"A hole!" Ripley pointed. "In the side of the nest!"

Barney hopped down from their perch and looked closely. There was a gap between the branches, about the size of a bowling ball.

Barney turned and spotted what was clearly a trail of

bent grass, a path, starting at the hole in question and leading down into the greeny thick of the forest.

"Oh my gosh," Barney said, looking through the hole
into the nest. "Do you think one of the eggs rolled out . . ."

Ripley was already bounding down a grassy hill, following the path deeper into the woods.

Egg! Egg! Egg! Egg!

By the time Barney caught up, Ripley was standing in
a sun patch of soft, leafy ferns next to a clearly unhatched
runaway egg.

A golden egg the size of a basketball.

Eggie!

In the sun, the egg looked like a magical glittery orb,
which cast a golden glow on Ripley's smiling face.

"It's Eggie!" Ripley cried, holding up her arms.

"It must have rolled out of the hole in the nest somehow," Barney mused. "Maybe it got knocked or pushed when the other eggs were hatching?"

"Maybe because he's small," Ripley said. "The mama bird didn't realize it could fall out of a hole."

"Small?" Barney raised their eyebrows. "This is a pretty big small egg."

"Eggie was the smallest of the eggs." Ripley wrapped her arms around the egg. "And now we have to protect him."

The egg was the temperature of a kitchen that had cookies baking in the oven. It warmed Ripley's cheek. "Don't worry, Eggie," she whispered. "I got you."

Barney looked up at the sky, spotted the sun, and made a quick calculation. "It's after breakfast," they said. "We have to get back. Or we're going to miss the theater workshop."

"But Eggie," Ripley whimpered, pointing.

"We'll come back during lunch," Barney said.

Eggie was so important, it didn't even occur to Ripley that she'd be missing two meals.

"Okay," she sighed.

Ripley grabbed Barney's hand, and the two bolted back to camp.

"I'll be back," Ripley called over her shoulder. "Don't go egg-ywhere!"

CHAPTER 8

"THE-AH-TAH!" Miss Panache, in an embroidered and bedazzled purple velvet smock and gold boots, strode back and forth in front of the assembled scouts, her hair high and frosted. "THE-A-TAH is a practice of MIND, BODY, and SOOOOOUL. Yes."

"Look at that hair," Mal sighed.

"Magical," Molly agreed.

"Yes," Jo added.

April nodded solemnly.

Jo wondered how big Miss Panache's closet was and whether she categorized her outfits by material: velvet, sequin, brocade, silk (and so on).

"And SO," Panache continued, reaching out into the crowd as though attempting to connect mind, body, and soul, "today we will begin by warming up all three by ACT-ING OUT. Yes. ACTING. OUT."

There is no hard science for how a person goes about pre-paring for theater creating. Panache's approach was certainly ODD, in the original nonacronym meaning of the word.

In their warm-up for the workshop, scouts ACTED like they were monkeys in a snowstorm, giraffes in a hailstorm, hedgehogs at the dentist, and, finally, octopuses having a tea party on a trampoline.

Bouncing and waggling her arms, Jo solidified her feel-ing that she was not cut out for the theater.

"I mean," Jo grumbled, as much as Jo could grumble, "REALLY. Explain the scientific justification of being an octopus."

Molly was equally embarrassed. Acting made Molly feel very exposed.

"Hey!" Ripley said, arriving as octopus bouncing hit a fever pitch. "What ARE you doing?"

"Acting." Molly blushed, wiggling her arms, her cheeks as red as cherries.

"Oh," Ripley said, wiggling her arms back at Molly, still worried about Eggie but also a little pleased to see everyone so bouncy.

"Where were you?" Molly asked. "You missed breakfast."

Before Ripley could answer, Miss Panache snapped her fingers.

"FAAABULOUS, FAAABULOUS," Miss Panache cooed. "Yes. Yes. Yes. I'm loving this and this, all of this. It's yes. It's now. It's a very successful warm-up, scouts. And NOW, gather with your groups and let your creative juices FLOW."

Now that all their muscles and souls were warmed up, team Goldi-Scout and the Three Bears gathered on a grassy spot just west of the mess hall and got down to the business of Show Business.

"I hope my soul and mind are warmed up," April noted.

Jo was happy to no longer be pretending. "I'm willing to risk it."

Ripley watched as April opened her notebook, which

was full of a night's worth of ideas, all laid out in sparkly pink pen.

Ripley liked watching April hatch her plans. Sometimes April reminded Ripley of her oldest sister, Amy, who always knew where people were supposed to sit at breakfast and who was allowed to watch what on TV.

Amy said Ripley had to sit at the end of the table because she was the littlest. And Amy thought table sitting should go by age. Which Ripley never understood, because what does age have to do with pancakes?

"Okay." April took one of the giant breaths that usually preceded her having a lot of ideas about something. "Okay, so I was thinking about this all night last night, and considering all the possible routes available, I was thinking maybe we need to do something BOLD, you know? So, I'm a huge fan of the Mermaid Lemonade Stand series— AREN'T WE ALL—and I realized, Holy Chita Rivera, this series would be a great way to approach Goldi-Scout and the Three Bears! And then I thought, we could do a whole thing as MERMAIDS!? *Under the Sea, Fanta-sea!* What do you think? Eh? Amazing, right?"

April paused and waited for everyone else to think it was a good idea.

A very good, big, complicated idea.

"Uh," Jo said, trying to imagine an underwater play.

"So, it's Goldi-Scout and the Three Bears, but the bears are mermaids?"

"Yes! And our HERO"—April waved her pencil in the air—"would be Annabella Goldi-Scout, underwater detective. DETECTING who slept in whose mermaid bed!"

Hes looked like her left eyeball was going to explode out of her face.

"Okay." Jo paused, sat back on the grass, and looked up at the sky like she was trying to picture it. "So, the whole play would be under . . . water?"

April nodded vigorously.

There was a tick or two of silence.

Finally, Hes, dressed in her hamburger hoodie (which is a hoodie with a picture of a hamburger on it and not a hoodie made of hamburger), pressed the heels of her hands against her eyes. "Man! This seems, like, REALLY complicated."

Like everything Roanoke did, Hes wanted to say, but didn't.

Hes wished she was playing basketball and not talking about plays.

"Uh." Wren raised her hand. "Why don't we just do the play, like, a regular play?"

Wren was moderately excited to be doing a play but wished it was a play about a goth girl who loved poetry and not a mermaid bear.

"Oh." April looked down at her notebook. "Yeah, I mean, y-yeah. I suppose we could just . . . do that . . ."

A soft silence fell over the group.

Ripley raised her hand to say something.

Ripley wanted to say that, actually, it wouldn't take Goldi-Scout long to figure out the mystery of who was sleeping in the MerBears' beds since, if her memory of the story was right, it was GOLDI-SCOUT herself who had done the sleeping, ending up in Baby Bear's perfect, not-too-soft bed. But before she could say anything, Miss Panache swooped in like a big purple velvet bird.

"GREETINGS, thespians," Miss Panache crooned. "I've been told to remind you that this work will help you earn your Get Your Act Together badge for playwriting, as well as the Acting Out (a.k.a. Nobody Knows I'm a Thespian) badge."

The scouts nodded, Panache thought, somewhat solemnly.

"Yes. Okay. I'm getting a sense. A feeling. What? What's happening here?" Panache waved her hands over Jo's and Hes's heads, stirring the air with her open palms. "You know what? I'm not getting a creative vibe from this group. I'm getting . . . a 'no.'"

April sighed. "We're just . . . having a little bit of discussion around the staging. Which, as we all know, is a crucial element of a play's success."

"Certainly, certainly." Miss Panache curled her finger under her chin. "Perhaps if you are stuck on staging, you could shift to the WHO of your play. WHO are your characters, what are their motivations? Yes?"

"Sure." Jo shrugged. "I mean, yes."

Miss Panache clapped her hands.

"Remember," Panache trilled, as she pranced off to the next group, "there are no small parts, only short plays! YES!"

Not far away, sopranos Susie Woo of Dartmoor and Sarah Smithereen of Woolpit—part of team The Scout Who Cried Wolf—were doing their best wolf impressions.

"AOOOOOOOOOOOOOOOOOOOO!" Susie trilled, holding her hands out.

"You know what? What if it was a growl?" Sarah stepped forward, rubbing her temples. "What if you sneered and went, like, GRRROOOOOOOOOOOO?"

Susie frowned and tugged on her braids. "That's not CRYING wolf."

"Right," Sarah said. "Well, try it in a middle C."

"AOOOOOOOOooooooooooooooooo!"

"Oh, I'm loving that," Sarah cooed, pressing her hands together. "That's a yes for me. Do THAT again."

"AOOOOOOOOooooooooooooooooo!"

"Okay," April sighed, flipping a page over in her notebook. "So, roles."

"I mean, I can be Mama Bear," Wren offered. "I have this super cool apron thing I could wear. It's got, like, a skull on it."

"I can be Papa Bear," Hes said.

"Shirley Prendergast, here's an idea." Jo smiled. "I can *not* be in the play. I can do the lighting and technical stuff."

Everyone looked at Ripley, who was actually thinking about eggsportation and the best way to move Eggie back to the nest.

"What part do you want, Rip?" April asked.

Ripley had kind of been expecting, ever since she found out they were doing Goldi-Scout, that she would be Baby Bear.

Ripley had been some version of Baby Bear ever since she was a baby. Because she was the Baby. The youngest. The smallest. All the time. No matter what.

She was a baby in all her siblings' games. She'd been a baby puppy and a baby kitten. She'd been a baby crying and a baby in a store. She'd been dress-up baby and even a unicorn baby.

She was also Baby Jesus at her grandma's church Christmas pageant every year. Even when the manger was a tight fit.

"I guess I'm the Baby Bear," she said.

"You don't have to be," April said. "I mean. You

can be Goldi-Scout. If you want. I mean, I could also be Goldi-Scout, because I'm older and Goldi-Scout is older . . ."

"Nah." Ripley shrugged. It felt so obvious that April was Goldi-Scout. That's who April WAS. "It's okay. I'll be Baby Bear."

"Okay, great!" April turned back to her notebook. "So, I'm Goldi-Scout. Now we just have to write it up, I guess."

"AOOOOOOOO°°°°°°°°°°°°°°°°°!"

"Well," Wren said, "maybe we should talk about how we want to change the story, because we get to change it, right? Maybe we don't have to use beds?"

Ripley blinked. Baby Bear had the perfect bed, she thought. Soft, but not too soft.

Just then, a smile spread across Ripley's face.

"Socks," she said to herself. "Socks!"

"Not LOCKS," April corrected, squinting as she scribbled new ideas into her notebook. "SCOUT. Goldi-SCOUT and the three everyday, run of the mill, perfectly ordinary bears."

CHAPTER 9

Fortunately, the pile of socks Mal had found under her bunk the day before was still sitting in front of Roanoke when Ripley rocketed back with a wheelbarrow and Barney in tow.

"How long is the rehearsal break?" Barney asked.

"Long enough to get to Eggie and back," Ripley promised. "'Cause I am Ripley and I am superfast!"

Ripley tossed the socks into the wheelbarrow, Barney climbed on board, and Ripley rocketed them back to the forest.

"What a great idea!" Barney smiled somewhat nervously, gripping the wheelbarrow tightly with both hands as they bumped and swayed, buffered by a pile of socks. "Hey, where did all these socks come from?"

"Feet," Ripley guessed, swerving to avoid a tree.

"It's a Lumberjane mystery!" she huffed. "Good thing is, now we can wrap Eggie in socks and wheelbarrow him up to the nest."

"Like an EGG ROLL!" Barney grinned as they ground to a halt in front of Eggie.

Who had not moved.

Because eggs, generally, can only roll down a hill.

And the nest was at least twenty feet away, uphill.

"EGGS-ACTLY!" Ripley tossed handfuls of socks into the air.

"So, why do you think Eggie is a him?" Barney wondered, jumping out of the wheelbarrow.

"Oh." Ripley looked at Eggie. "Maybe it's not. I mean, Eggie is an egg. It could be a her!"

"Or. Maybe Eggie is a they," Barney offered. "You know . . . like me."

"WHUT!" Ripley said, smiling at Barney. "That would be SO COOL."

"Sure," Barney said. "Eggie can be just . . . Eggie!"

"Eggie is Eggie," Ripley agreed. "YES!"

Barney grinned, twirling their fingers in the air like Miss Panache. "YES! I'm feeling this. YES!"

It took a while to lift Eggie into the wheelbarrow and pack Eggie up with mismatched socks and then another effort to roll the wheelbarrow up the relatively steep incline back to the nest.

Getting Eggie through the hole Eggie had rolled out of also proved to be a bit tricky. For one, the hole wasn't really a hole but a gap created when one of the branches in the nest had cracked, just enough to create a space the size of Eggie.

Generally, it is harder to get something back in than to pour something out. Which anyone who has ever poured too much milk on their cereal knows.

"One, two, three, PUSH!" Ripley growled. And with a large shove, Eggie popped back into the nest.

"Do you think Eggie's mom will come back?" Ripley panted as they rolled Eggie to the center of the nest.

"Actually," Barney noted, "since both mothers and fathers of various species perform the role of caring for unhatched eggs, it could be the dad who comes back. Like, with seahorses, the female lays the eggs, and the male looks after them."

"What if Eggie is a giant baby seahorse?!" Ripley gasped.

"Now THAT would be something," Barney said. "The key is to observe what does happen instead of deciding what you think should happen."

"That's a science thing," Ripley said, unsure.

"That's a life thing." Barney winked.

Once Eggie was resettled in the nest, Ripley couldn't help but think the nest looked pretty bare without Eggie's recently hatched siblings. Like a single cookie on a plate, Eggie looked a little . . . lonely.

"Maybe we should keep the socks on Eggie," she said, touching the top of Eggie gently. "In case Eggie gets cold."

"Actually, this nest is pretty warm," Barney said, holding out their hand to test the temperature. "Which is kind of fascinating, given that there's not an actual heat source in the nest. Maybe there's something in the shells that has some sort of thermal quality. Anyway, we need to leave the nest as close to the way we found it as possible, so the parent doesn't get scared off. Even though we've already broken the Do Not Disturb rule, we don't want to disturb any more than we have to."

Ripley looked at Eggie. "Sorry, Eggie," she said quietly.

"We should get back," Barney said, stepping up onto the edge of the nest.

"Okay," Ripley sighed.

Ripley leaned forward and looked Eggie in the part of the shell that she guessed would be Eggie's eyes.

"Okay, Eggie," she said quietly. "We have to go. But you're going to be okay. Even if it gets dark. You can always sing yourself an egg song. And pretty soon your parent will come back for you. Maybe with all your siblings. And I'm going to come back and visit you every day until they do."

"Bye, Eggie," Barney called, hopping over the edge of the nest.

Ripley leaned in closer. "I was the last egg too," she whispered. "Don't worry. It's going to be okay."

As Ripley turned away, she could have sworn she heard a small *tick-ticking* sound. Like a little claw on a teacup.

But when she looked back, Eggie was just sitting there. Still.

After Ripley and Barney left, the purple of evening turned into the black of night over the nest.

Alone in the dark, Eggie might have heard a little *hoo-hooing* from a bird in the tree branch above it. Or a skittering of squirrel claws on branches. A snuffling of a passing skunk looking for a meal of berries and grubs.

If Eggies could hear.

If so, late into the night, Eggie would also have heard all that noise stop, as if the forest itself were pausing, listening.

To the sound of an approaching intruder.

A whizzing sound, the squeak of a wheel. A sharp voice.

A hand slipped out from in between the bushes, followed by a hat, and a head.

"Coast is clear," the voice said. "COME ON, EUGENE! LET'S GO!"

CHAPTER 10

The Lumberjanes, since their founding a very very very long time ago, have had a very interesting history of performance and performance art.

In the early days, most plays were instructional demonstrations, focused on safety and the best way to, say, milk a goat. Over time, larger productions became popular, including a run of the Shakespeare's Feminist Sister theater company, which produced a string of hits including *Julia Cesar*, starring Julia "The Boxer" Gadolinium Maybelle Cesar.

That night, after dinner, April curled up in her bunk with her notebook and scratched away at possible insightful dialogue for Goldi-Scout and the Three (Nonmermaid) Bears.

So far she had,

Well, look at this very nice ~~house~~ cottage! I wonder who lives here.

One line. Which she hated. I mean, was it a cottage? Did it have to be?

Jo headed to the library to look up books on theatrical lighting.

Mal and Molly spent the night practicing their new parts on their favorite picnic table with their favorite snacks, apples and marshmallows.

"Okay," Molly said, finally shaking out her fingers. "We need to stop. I feel like we've been playing for hours."

"We sort of have been," Mal said. "Isn't it awesome! I love getting it right when it just plays and you don't have to think about it."

"I feel like I'm finally getting better," Molly said, looking at her accordion, with its pearly finish. "Like I can actually do this? You know? Like no one at home would believe it if I told them I was playing an instrument!"

"You're so good," Mal said, biting into her apple. "I still think we should start a band! Wouldn't that be cool?"

"Would we have to sing in front of people?" Molly wondered, her cheeks getting hot.

"Yes," Mal said. "But it would still be amazing."

"What would we call the band?" Molly said, resting her chin on her accordion.

"How about *The Radioactive Scout Project?*" Mal offered. "Or *Indigo MENACE.* Or—"

"Hmmm," Molly said, trying to picture it in her head. She couldn't see it. All she could see was the Molly who would never do that sort of thing.

"CAMPERS!" Jen's voice cut into the night. "LIGHTS OUT IN TEN!"

"Tomorrow," Mal said, hopping off the bench. "Tomorrow I'm going to write our first song. And we can play it in the play. I'll write a BEASTLY BALLAD!"

"You ever notice the little songs Ripley sings?" Molly asked, looking at her sneakers glowing white against the dark nighttime grass as they walked back to the cabin. "She's always singing these little songs."

"About what?" Mal asked, looking up at the crowded sky.

"I think . . . eggs," Molly said. "I think I heard eggs . . ."

"Was Ripley at dinner tonight?" Mal asked, as they got closer to the cabin.

"She was, but she was really quiet," Molly said, "and she only had one hot dog."

"Well, that's weird. Do you think she's nervous about doing a play?" Mal wondered.

"I don't think so," Molly said. "Do you think she'll be Baby Bear?"

"I mean, she kind of IS Baby Bear, right? She's all cuddly

and cute and sweet?" Mal held up her arms like she was giving a Baby Bear a big hug.

Back in the cabin, April lay on her bed, glaring at her notebook like it was a rainy day.

"It's just such a dumb story," she groaned. "So. Some kid breaks into a house and eats some bears' food and sleeps in their beds? And the Papa Bear has a hard bed and the Mama Bear has a soft bed? These are stereotypes! How is this an interesting play? I'll tell you what—it's NOT, and I think it would be better if we could make it underwater, even though I know . . ."

"Can't do it," Jo said, not looking up from her book. "Yes."

"It's not very ODD," Ripley said, curled up in her bunk. "Going into a bear house."

April leaned out over her bed. "ODD?"

"You're not supposed to disturb an animal's home," Ripley said, solemnly. "Observe. Document. Do *Not* Disturb."

"That's right." Jo, who was well read on the scientific process, including the ODD approach, looked up, surprised. "When did you start reading Miss Jane Petunia Massy Acorn Dale?"

"When I met Eggie," Ripley said. "And Barney told me about it."

"Eggie?" April dropped her notebook and sat up in bed. "Hey," she said, looking at Ripley, "Were you saying something about—"

Just then, Mal and Molly walked in the door, followed by Jen, tapping her watch.

"Lights out in two minutes!" Jen said, collapsing onto her bunk. "We're going to bed at a reasonable hour tonight. Sleep is golden."

"What's a reasonable hour?" Jo wondered, genuinely.

"Now is a reasonable hour," Jen noted, snapping off the lights. "Goodnight, scouts."

"GOODNIGHT, JEN!" everyone whispered loudly.

CHAPTER 11

By the time the half-moon was high in the sky like half of a pie, everyone in the cabin was asleep.

Except for Ripley.

This was strange, because Ripley was normally exhausted. From bouncing. But tonight, there was a little pain in Ripley's chest. A tender spot where she just felt . . . sad. Sad for Eggie.

Imagine being in a big family of eggs and then one day you're alone in your nest. With nothing but shells.

There is actually a movie about this, about a kid whose parents left him all by himself in his house over Christmas. It was Ripley's least favorite movie.

Lying in her bunk, curled around her favorite stuffed

toy, Mr. Sparkles, Ripley could picture Eggie. Eggie was not snuggled in a cabin, surrounded by friends, in a fluffy sleeping bag, with a night-light. Eggie was surrounded by dark, in the woods, alone.

"Do you think Eggie is scared?" she whispered to Mr. Sparkles.

Mr. Sparkles looked back at Ripley with sad button eyes.

"Me too," Ripley whispered.

At home, Ripley shared a room with her sister, who snored and talked in her sleep. At camp, she shared a room with the members of Roanoke, who also snored. So Ripley could sleep through just about anything.

But the idea of Eggie sleeping alone put a pit in her stomach and kept her eyes wide open.

Ripley had never slept alone. There was always someone close enough to grab if she had a bad dream.

Eggie had never slept alone either, Ripley thought.

Ripley slipped out from under the covers.

"Let's go keep Eggie company," she whispered to Mr. Sparkles.

With Mr. Sparkles and her blanket tucked under one arm, she grabbed her sneakers and, unnoticed, crept out the door.

CHAPTER 12

Night in the forest has its own unique soundtrack. *Chirp-chirping* becomes a long, echoing *hoo-hoo*. Sharp barks give way to distant howls.

Somewhere in this forest, on this particular dark night, there was the soft squitchy sound of rubber boot on mud.

Rosie ran her flashlight over the ground, unconcerned with the noises around her. The noises around her were noises she knew well. Noises of the dark. Rosie's concern was for the footprints pressed into the mucky forest floor.

For several days now, Rosie—who, of course, had her Right on Track badge (because she had almost every badge a scout could have; including a few no one had ever heard

of)—had been keeping tabs on the comings and goings of several sets of prints in the woods outside of camp.

Of course, this being a forest, there were lots of tracks; there was the common double lima bean of the caribou track, the skinny long fingers of the raccoon print. In addition, each scout had their own specific patterns and gaits that Rosie had learned to identify over the years.

Lately, though, there were new prints. These were a concerning sight, these footprints, even more concerning than the very large three-toed tracks she'd spotted in the woods many days earlier. These tracks were shoe tracks, human tracks; two sets of shoe prints—human, one deep, one shallow—she'd noticed first on the edge of the forest. And a single track, a tire track, that wiggled between the prints like a dizzy beeline.

Rosie bent over and picked up a wrapper next to a smudged footprint. Sniffing the paper, she detected a faint whiff of artificial flavoring.

"Beef Gravy Double Bubble Gum," she mused. "Interesting."

"INTERESTING?!" growled a voice behind her. "HOW ABOUT LITTERING?"

"Hello, you old coot," Rosie said, pocketing the piece of paper and spinning around, just as the woman the scouts called Bearwoman, which was not her actual name, shifted shapes from Bear into grouchy old woman.

Who today was covered in burrs.

"You get stuck in the brush?" Rosie asked. "You're looking a little burrier than usual."

"Keep laughin', Red," Bearwoman huffed, picking the spiny plants off her tattered coat. "Once again, the borders of the camp are trespassed and you do nothing."

"I would think by now you'd see that I'm very much aware of what's going on, and I am very much taking care of things," Rosie said. "Maybe not to YOUR standards—"

"No, NOT to my standards," Bearwoman interrupted, pushing up against Rosie so they were standing nose to nose (sort of, maybe more like chin to face). "But then, you are well aware of that."

"I am," Rosie said, taking a step back and pulling a burr off her shirt. "As much as I appreciate this visit, and the ongoing assessment of my performance as camp director, and I do . . . the eggs hatched. So we should be fine."

Bearwoman scrunched up her face. "HUMPH! *Should* be. *Should* is for suckers."

Rosie lifted her head and sniffed the air. Though she wasn't keen to get into it with her, Bearwoman was right. There was definitely something afoot.

77

"Someone is here," Bearwoman said. "*They* are here."

"And we will deal with *them*," Rosie said. "If and when the moment arises. But as I said, the eggs have hatched."

"We shall see about that," Bearwoman said before rumbling off into the woods.

Suddenly, there was a cry, a human cry, from the edge of the forest.

Rosie's blood chilled two degrees.

She turned and started to run in the direction of the voice in the dark, which was crying out, "IT'S GONE! EGGIE! EGGIE IS GONE!"

PART TWO

RIGHT ON TRACK
THE TRACKS OF YOUR PEERS

Through rain, or snow, or the cold wind . . . a scout with this badge must demonstrate the ability to not only identify but also, successfully and undetected, trail a variety of birds and animals through their natural habitats using only the prints they leave in their wake.

A scout with this badge can glance at the forest floor and determine the foot traffic, or flights, of the many creatures come and gone.

To understand the meaning of a creature's mark is to understand a complex history of adaptation, migration, and . . .

CHAPTER 13

Ripley kneeled in the nest, the sharp edges of the wood digging into her knees, her heart beating so hard, it felt like it was going to break out of her chest like a cannonball.

Eggie was gone.

A sob filled her throat, made her nose prickle, her eyes hot.

GONE!

And Eggie hadn't rolled out a little hole in the nest like last time.

Someone had cut right through the side of the nest. The way you cut a piece of pie when you're taking a really big piece and not leaving a lot of pie for the next person.

Just looking at the cut edges of the branches made Ripley's heart hurt.

"Eggie," she whispered, rubbing her face into Mr. Sparkles, clutched to her chest. "Oh, Eggie."

Suddenly there was a light, bobbing in the dark. Boots on mud.

Kalop! Kalop! Kalop! Kalop!

"Ripley?" Rosie called out into the night. "Is that you?"

"Yes," Ripley croaked back.

Rosie reached the edge of the nest and rubbed the fog off her glasses. "What happened?"

"S-s-someone stole Eggie," Ripley whimpered.

"STOLE egg?" a gruff voice growled from behind Rosie.

Bearwoman materialized next to Rosie and adjusted her spectacles. "What egg? I was *told* the eggs had hatched."

"I thought they had," Rosie said, looking into the nest. "They had."

"There was"—Ripley's eyes started to well up with hot little tears—"an egg. A last egg. It r-rolled out of the nest."

Ripley pointed to where she and Barney had chased after Eggie. "Barney and me brought Eggie back. And we p-put it here. So the parent could come."

"And it appears," Bearwoman growled under her breath, "that something else has come instead. As might have been predicted. If anyone was paying attention."

Rosie stepped up into the nest and put her hand on Ripley's back. "It's okay, scout. Take a deep breath."

Ripley shook her head. "N-not okay."

Bearwoman ran a finger over the edge of the sliced nest. "We need to start looking . . . NOW. They can't have gotten far."

Bearwoman turned and took a step back from the hole that had been cut into the side of the nest. She bent over and pressed her palms, which were sometimes paws, into the mud and sniffed.

"Gravy," she muttered. "Beef Gravy Double-Bubble Bubble Gum. We know what that means."

Also. There were the prints. Shoe prints. Not unlike the ones Rosie had spotted days earlier.

Just then, there was another rustling in the trees, through which burst a very worried April and Jo.

"Hey!" April called out, her face full of worry. "What happened?"

"Ripley," Jo said, quietly, "are you okay?"

The other members of Roanoke burst through the trees, trailed by Jen, who was wishing that her scouts would spend one, ONE, night peacefully slumbering in their beds and not disappearing.

"Ripley!" Molly cried, jumping into the nest and bundling Ripley up into her arms. "Are you okay?"

Ripley shook her head.

"The Order. They have taken the egg," Bearwoman snapped, wagging a finger at Rosie.

Bubbles crawled down from Molly's head and wrapped himself around Ripley's neck like a blanket.

Jen shone her flashlight into the nest. "What's going on?"

Rosie stepped out of the nest, careful to avoid the tracks Bearwoman had pointed to. "Jen, I need you to take these scouts back to their cabin."

Jen nodded, only a little shocked to hear her name come out of Rosie's mouth. Which meant things must be particularly serious.

"What's happening?" Mal asked.

"Eggie," Ripley mumbled, from inside the muffle of Bubbles's fur.

"Eggie," April repeated.

"Gone," Ripley said into Bubbles's fuzz.

"Don't worry about it. We'll take care of it," Rosie said. "Just go back to bed."

Jo tried to take in as much as she could see with the beam of her flashlight.

"Okay, scouts," Jen said, her voice as serious as Rosie's. "Back to the cabin."

Molly wrapped her arm around Ripley and walked her out of the nest. "Come on, Ripley."

Ripley buried her head in Molly's shoulder.

"I promised," she sniffed, tears running down her cheeks.

"I know," Molly said, squeezing Ripley as they slowly moved away from the empty nest, the place where Eggie once was.

"We need to fix this," Bearwoman growled.

Falling forward onto her front feet as her body shifted back into bear form, she pressed her nose to the ground.

"I know," Rosie said.

Pushing her glasses up her nose and looking up into the night sky, she felt a small twist of very un-Rosie-like worry. "I know."

CHAPTER 14

The next morning, even when Kzyzzy came by with a stack of cornmeal waffles topped with blueberries and whipped cream, Ripley wasn't hungry.

And Ripley was always, like, ALWAYS hungry, even when most people were no longer even thinking about the possibility of food. When most people would say it would be physically impossible to keep eating, Ripley had another pancake.

It was what Ripley did, reliably and certainly.

But not that morning.

That morning, Ripley had NO pancakes. Zero. NONE.

Not even one of those little pancakes the size of a dime that accidentally get made when you make regular pancakes.

That morning, all Ripley would eat was a slice of orange. And even that she nibbled without a drop of zest or zeal.

It was almost like Ripley wasn't Ripley that morning. Like if you saw her sitting at the table you would lean forward and introduce yourself to this noneating, unhappy little scout.

Molly rubbed Ripley's back, which is what Molly knew to do when people were sad. That and get glasses of water, which is something lots of people do when people are sad, although no scientific study that Jo had ever read suggested a glass of water did anything for feeling sad.

April did what April knew to do when people are sad, which is talk about how things could possibly get much better than they are now.

And they could be, in April's estimation, because Rosie and Bearwoman were on the case.

"I mean, Holy Serena and Venus Williams," April gushed. "You want to talk about dynamic duos? You want to talk about who you want on a case like this? I mean, this is what Rosies do, right? They come in and kind of already know what's going on?"

"Like Angela Lansbury," Jo noted.

"YES! I mean"—April held her fingers together in a tiny pinch pose—"I heard Rosie once found a grain of sand in a barrel of rice. I heard she once found a pearl at the bottom of the INKY WINKY Sea, with her eyes closed!"

Ripley thought an egg is not a grain of sand, and a dark forest is not a barrel of rice.

"I bet you they find that egg so fast, you don't even notice it's missing," April said, crossing her arms with a sharp nod.

"Except"—April put a finger to her lips—"I guess you already know it's missing. BUT you won't know for LONG, I guess that's what I'm saying. Right. Like ANY MINUTE now Rosie and Bearwoman are going to come charging in here with Eggie, and you'll FORGET you ever were missing Eggie, THAT's what I'm saying."

Jo watched April catch her breath.

Ripley kept her eyes on the orange slice on her plate.

Everyone waited for Ripley to say something.

"I have a stomachache," she said, finally, pushing back from the table.

Saying you have a stomachache is a way of saying you're really sad and worried when it's hard to say you're sad and worried.

Scouts were emptying out of their seats and heading to Theater Workshop.

"Okay, well," Jo said, "I'll come check on you later, okay?"

Ripley nodded. She took small sad steps to the door, the most un-Ripley-like steps Jo had ever seen.

Inside the cabin, Ripley climbed up to her bed and sat down next to Mr. Sparkles.

"What do I do?"

She tried lying down, but lying down seemed to make everything even more sad, like lying down was dumping all the sad directly into her brain.

So she sat up.

A Ripley thing to do would be to sing. This is how Ripleys normally think and fill the air when it's quiet.

But when Ripley opened her mouth to sing, nothing came out.

There was no song in Ripley's heart that morning.

Not even a note.

Not even a little one.

Another Ripley thing to do would be to bounce, but Ripley didn't have any bounce in her either. She didn't even want to stand up. Her arms felt like they weighed a hundred pounds.

It was the least bouncy Ripley had ever felt.

"What do I do?" she repeated to herself, so quietly the words barely left her lips.

All Ripley wanted to do was save Eggie from whatever had taken Eggie out of its nest. But no one seemed to think that was a Ripley thing to do. April thought it was a Rosie thing.

But the idea of saving Eggie was the only thing that filled her heart.

Ripley turned and looked at Mr. Sparkles.

"Eggie is OUT there, Mr. Sparkles!"

Mr. Sparkles was propped up so he looked like he was sitting with one hoof under his chin, gazing at Ripley with attentive button eyes.

It seemed to Ripley that if any of her fellow cabinmates had found Eggie and lost Eggie, they would go to help Eggie. That would be what Jo would do; that's definitely what April would do. And Mal and Molly.

Even if Rosie was on the case.

They wouldn't be sitting in the cabin with a stomachache they didn't even really have.

Why can't you help Eggie? Mr. Sparkles seemed to wonder with his little yarn mouth turned down slightly.

This is a very Lumberjane question, incidentally.

Lumberjanes do not ask, why? They ask, why not?

Ripley squished her face up with determination.

"I will save Eggie!"

Ripley slammed her fist into her hand, which was something she had seen April do many times before April did something.

Moments later, Ripley bounced into Zodiac cabin, where Barney was sitting with a book on their lap. Because

Barney, who had heard about Eggie, and who also didn't actually enjoy doing Butoh, also had "a stomachache."

"BARNEY!" Ripley announced. "I don't know how, but we need to go save Eggie."

"YES, WE DO!" Barney slammed their book shut. Because that was exactly what Barney had been thinking ever since Vanessa told them what had happened.

"YES, WE DO!" Ripley cheered, because it felt good to cheer.

Barney paused. "What should we do?"

Ripley squeezed her eyes shut and tried to think.

Ripley wondered if, when some people were asked to think of something, they looked into their heads and found a box full of ideas. Ripley did not see a box of ideas. I mean, there was STUFF in there, lots of stuff (like pictures of unicorns and a list of her favorite cereals, cartoons, and dance moves), just not the things she imagined other people saw, like plans and maps and useful stuff like that.

Ripley sighed. "I don't know," she said quietly.

A tiny thought occurred to Ripley. Maybe the reason some people were the kinds of people who could save people and some people weren't was BECAUSE some people had filing cabinets in their brains and some didn't.

Maybe that meant Ripley couldn't save Eggie.

Barney held up a finger.

"We know how to observe!" they noted. "*And* I've been reading up about TRACKS! Why don't we go back to the nest and see if we can see anything that maybe Rosie and Bearwoman missed!"

THAT sounded like the beginning of a plan.

"Hurray!" Ripley cheered. "Back to the nest!"

CHAPTER 15

The Miss Qiunzella Thiskwin Penniquiqul Thistle Crumpet's Camp for Hardcore Lady-Types Library is much like every other library, in that it contains many books categorized by subject, smells like old paper, and is run by a very knowledgeable librarian who hates noise but loves heavy metal music.

It is also NOT like most other libraries, in that it is also a ship.

There were many rumors around camp about how it was that a very large ship came to be in the northern part of the camp, very near the camp director's cabin.

There was one rumor that the ship was built on a dare, by several scouts looking to get their Float Your Boat badge.

The other was that it was dropped when a creature who was supposed to deliver the boat to the lake sneezed and, accidentally, released the ship from its claws.

Apparently, after dropping the boat, the creature became embarrassed and flew away.

That's the rumor, anyway.

Either way, this library, like any other library, was a place for any Lumberjane who was looking to learn something about something. Especially for those Lumberjanes who liked learning from books. Especially Lumberjanes who liked really OLD books.

Which, to be fair, formerly, was NOT Jo.

For a long time, Jo preferred databases to old books, because Jo used to think old books smelled funny (and databases did not).

But then she became a Lumberjane and April introduced her to the beauty of yellowy pages and little scratches in ink and all the cool things people write in really old books, and Jo was won over.

People can change.

(Books cannot, but that's another thing altogether.)

That day, Jo was in the library looking up information on wiring, in preparation for the grand production of Goldi-Scout and the Three Bears, currently being rehearsed, which, thankfully, was still taking place on dry land, last time Jo checked.

Jo was very very happy that she'd found a job working on the production elements of the play and not on the stage.

The production elements of the play are actually just as important as the play, which you would know if you took all of them away and tried to watch a play without them.

Which you would be doing, for one, in the dark, because LIGHTS are a big part of theater production.

Which got Jo thinking about HOW she could light up the stage for the play.

This is another good Lumberjane question, by the way: HOW?

This led Jo down the path of researching the history of limelight, which, as a word, can be defined as a state of being under public examination and also as a way that people in the olden days lit up a stage, using limestone.

Jo had done previous experiments with limestone as a child, as she had once imagined all children did until she met other kids and realized not everyone had a lab when they were three.

Jo was wondering whether it would be worth trying to do something with limestone or if she should just invent some new, possibly solar-powered lighting mechanism when she stumbled upon something she wasn't looking for.

Which is what often happens in a library. Where books all hang out together in rows and are sometimes left on desks and tables.

In this case, the thing Jo stumbled upon was a very old and very big book that someone had been rifling through earlier and then left open on top of a stack of other books.

THE VERY BIG BOOK OF CURIOUS PEOPLE

The Very Big Book of Curious People was a work in progress, part of the Lumberjanes Anthropolo-ME badge, which encouraged scouts to go out into the world and learn, again, ODDly, about the various peoples they discovered there.

Researcher Miss Jane Petunia Massy Acorn Dale had committed several pieces to this big book, including a brief section on a community of very tall people passionate about three-day cruises and espressos.

Jo, who was an Acorn Dale fan, did not know this.

But still, the book was . . . curious to her.

"Hmmm," Jo said. "This looks interesting."

Prior to Jo's arrival at the library, another person had been looking through *The Very Big Book of Curious People* very deliberately, as opposed to accidentally. This person had flipped to the back of the book to the index, which is a part of the book that lists which topics can be found where in a book.

This book that you are reading, unfortunately, has no index, but if it did, it would read:

EGG: 5, 7, 15, 16, 26, 30, 37, 38, 39, 42, 43, 44,
45, 48, 50, 51, 54, 59, 61, 62, 63, 64, 65, 68,
69, 70, 71, 72, 73, 77, 78, 85, 86, 87, 88, 92,
93, 94, 95, 101, 102, 103, 105, 109, 112, 113,
114, 122, 123, 126, 127, 128, 129, 138, 146,
147, 149, 150, 151, 152, 153, 154, 158, 159,
165, 166, 167, 168, 170, 171, 173, 174, 175,
182, 183, 184, 185, 186, 188, 189, 190, 191,
192, 193, 194, 195, 196, 198, 199, 203
LIBRARY: 14, 40, 67, 97, 98, 100, 101, 103

The Very Big Book of Curious People had three entries under EGG.

The Egg on Your Face Society, a group of big-bellied biologists who became obsessed with the possibility of reversing the aging process with intensive yolk treatments.

The Knights of the Round Egg, a group of knights who enjoyed sitting around tables shaped like eggs and playing cards (and not much else if we're honest).

And.

The Order of the Golden Egg.

This egg-oriented entry was the entry that the last reader had left the book open to, before camp duties had summoned them away. And so this egg entry was the first thing Jo saw, as she placed her stack of books, which was very tall at this point, down, and took a closer look.

"The Order of the Golden Egg," Jo read aloud, in a quiet, library-appropriate whisper.

Jo tapped her chin. Hadn't Bearwoman said something about an order?

She closed her eyes.

Yes. She had. "The Order has the egg," she'd said.

Above the entry was a photo of a bunch of very grim-looking people, all wearing what seemed to be white bands around their foreheads and some kind of long underwear.

Underneath, the text read:

The Order of the Golden Egg is a very curious society of egg enthusiasts who believe that golden eggs hold the ability to grant them wealth and power and make them popular with popular people. The members of the Order of the Golden Egg are renowned for their artisanal eggcups and infamous for their habit of stealing eggs, especially golden eggs, from nests in the wild. Also, they have terrible taste in clothes, music, transportation, and food. The Order was outlawed for their egg stealing, but literature on the power of the Golden Egg surfaced in the late 1900s, suggesting they have moved their activities underground.

"Well, that is legitimately curious," Jo said. "And timely."

Slamming the book shut, Jo dashed out of the library and was immediately shushed by Cornillia Sprint, the librarian.

"Great Elizabeth Freeman," she hissed. "This is a place of LEARNING! So, SHHHHH!"

"Sorry," Jo whispered as she slipped out the door and off to find Ripley.

CHAPTER 16

The process by which an idea becomes a play is complex and magical and also, at times, extremely frustrating.

In the olden days, audiences would attend theaters with baskets of old and rotting fruit that they would throw at the cast if they were at all displeased with the performance.

Which they often were.

For most people involved in theater, though, this is nothing compared to the headache involved in just *writing* a play.

Writing a play is like pulling something—an idea or even a whole world—out of your head, even when that thing isn't in there in the first place.

Which, truly, for April, was kind of the case in the case of Goldi-Scout. Writing a play was not like writing Mermaid mystery fan fiction and it was not like climbing a mountain. Nor was it like playing basketball or inventing a rocket ship, all things that seemed way more fun than Goldi-Scout.

Which was NOT FUN.

Shockingly.

But it was the task given to April (by April), and so she did it. Because that's what Lumberjanes do, April reasoned.

Also, as Annabella Panache had said many times, "The SHOW must go on, YES!"

And so, with everyone gathered for Theater Workshop, sitting just beyond the picnic benches on the green grass under a bright, hopeful blue sky, April handed out copies of the script she had written to Hes and Wren.

It was not her best script. It was not even the fifth best thing she had ever written, but at least it was something, and they wouldn't get any further off schedule.

"Oh, you wrote it already," Hes said, taking the page. "Huh."

"Ripley has a stomachache, so I'll play Baby Bear as well today," April added.

"Is she okay?" Wren asked, through a veil of purple hair.

"She's really sad about Eggie," April said.

Hes nodded. "Yeah, Barney told us. I hope they find it."

April sighed, flipping over the first page of the script. "Okay. So, this is ACT 1: A COTTAGE, where we set the scene . . . and stuff."

Hes looked down at the piece of paper in her hand. Then up at April. "So, um, what's my motivation?"

"Oh." April looked at the script. "Well, someone's broken into your house. And it's your Bear house. So, it's important. And you're the Papa Bear, and you notice that someone's been eating your . . . oatmeal . . . and . . ."

It was a rare thing for April to hear herself talking and be completely unenthused by what she was saying.

"Sorry, guys." April sighed, dropping her pages with a *FFLUP*. "I'm maybe a little uninspired with this particular piece. Yes. I mean, I want this to be the greatest play ever and it CAN be, obviously, the greatest play ever I just . . . I thought it would be cool to make the play underwater, but obviously that's too complicated and we would need a lot of water and that's probably pretty wasteful and I totally get that but I guess I couldn't think of a way to make this interesting if it's not underwater which is not to say it's not interesting I just . . . ran out of ideas."

Hes looked up at April to see if she was finished talking. Sometimes it was hard to tell. Currently, April was very still, her head down. Like someone had taken just a little too much air out of the April balloon.

"Um. Okay. Well." Hes grabbed a long piece of grass and put it between her teeth, chewing and thinking. "Maybe we can figure it out together. I mean, it's a group thing, right?"

Chewing on grass is how Heses think, incidentally.

Hes looked at the script some more. "I think my Papa Bear is a stay-at-home dad."

April raised her head. "That's a good idea."

"Sure." Hes pulled a pencil out from her pocket and wrote some notes on her script. "So it's even more messed up, right, that this scout came into my house, because I just cleaned up. And it's hard for a bear to be a stay-at-home dad because it's like, it's not well understood as a real job in the bear community, right? Maybe there are other bears that don't support my choices."

Wren, who had also come with a pencil, tapped hers against her lips. "I think Mama Bear is really dissatisfied with her job and so she feels like this is a chance to express her anger."

"Oh." April looked down at her script, which had significantly fewer stars and hearts in the margins than usual.

She took out a pencil and drew a little flower in the top corner of her page. "I mean . . . We could do that. We're retelling, right? Just because the roles are written kind of boring, they don't have to stay that way. Even if we're not doing mermaids. Which I get, we're not."

"So." Hes tugged on her baseball cap. "Maybe this is just one in a bunch of frustrating days for the Bears, you know? Maybe we could play it that way."

April considered. "Yeah. And then maybe it's a bad day for Goldi-Scout too! I mean, why else would she be going into some strange bear's house? That's super un-scout of her!"

"Hey, what if Goldi-Scout doesn't even want to be GOLDI-SCOUT?" Hes offered. "Maybe she wants to be, like, a PINK-HAIRED basketball-playing scout? Maybe she's only in the bears' house because she wants to find some people to play basketball with or something?"

April smiled. "Yeah! Why not?"

Wren looked at her script. "Why don't we just improvise a scene? Improv is an acting thing, right? Like we could start with our motivations and then just see what plays out?"

"That's a great idea." April grinned. "We need to give Baby Bear some stuff too."

"Yeah, Baby Bear." Wren tapped her lips with her fingers. "I don't really get her motivation. Other than finding Goldi-Scout . . ."

"Baby Bear." April looked at her script. "Is the Bear . . . that tells you . . . something is wrong . . ."

Right then, Hen looked up and pointed. "Hey, here comes Jo. Wow. She's running."

"Running?" April looked off into the distance. Jo *was* running. Sprinting, even. Jo, who was very tall and could walk very fast, rarely ran unless there was a reason to.

"HEY!" Jo skidded to a stop next to the group. "Where's Ripley?"

April frowned. "She's in the cabin with a stomachache."

Jo shook her head. "No, she's not. The cabin is empty. Barney's gone too. I think they've gone looking for Eggie, who I also think was kidnapped by this group of really tacky egg-obsessed people called the Order of the Golden Egg."

April clapped her hands to her cheeks. "HOLY Roberta Bondar!"

"Okay." Hes stood up, brushing grass off her jacket. "Let's go."

"LET'S go?" April said, scrambling to her feet.

"Right, I mean"—Hes frowned—"you guys are going to go do something to help someone, and it's going to end up being cool and we want to help too."

"Yeah," Wren nodded. "You guys are always the ones

running off into the woods to do cool stuff! Plus, what if Barney needs our help?"

"Sounds good," Jo said, looking over her shoulder. "Okay. SO, I think if they're anywhere, they're back at that nest."

"Do you know where that is?" Wren asked, twisting her purple hair around her finger.

"Yes, we do." April nodded. "Looks like it's Lumber-janes to the rescue!!"

"Oh"—Hes raised a finger—"there's one more thing we should probably grab."

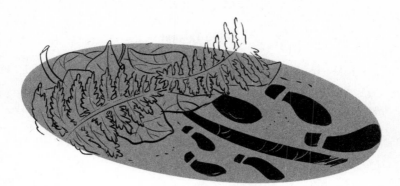

CHAPTER 17

By the time Ripley and Barney arrived at the nest, the ground around it was trampled to mush.

"It looks like there's been quite a few creatures here," Barney said, consulting their *Scouts Guide to Tracking*. "Deer tracks, rabbit tracks, and I think these are Rosie's."

Barney walked over to the west side of the nest and looked closely at the ground. "I think I can still see the tracks they followed away from the nest. Do you think we should follow them?"

Ripley was standing in the nest, trying very hard to observe and not be upset.

Which is hard, because being upset can be a very big thing to be.

Ripley took a deep breath.

> *Oh Egg Oh*
> *Where did you go*
> *Who took you away*
> *To my dismay*

Ripley turned and sang.

> *You're just an egg*
> *You don't have a leg*
> *So*
> *Someone must have*
> *Carried you . . .*

(Not all songs have to rhyme.)

As she sang, Ripley had a thought, which happens when Ripleys are singing. Maybe, she thought, part of observing could be not just looking at things but looking to see what was DIFFERENT from before.

Ripley blinked. The nest was different, but not different from how it was the night before, when someone had sawed a chunk out of the front of it.

What else? Ripley thought. What else is different?

Hopping out of the nest, Ripley walked over to the east side of the nest, eyeing the ground, careful not to step on anything important, on anything that could be a clue or a sign, anything that could be something she hadn't spotted earlier.

As she stepped to the north side of the nest, she spotted it: a trail, not of tracks, but of broad flat leaves, leaves that didn't look like they belonged around the nest and definitely weren't there the day before. They looked like leaves from the ferns that she had found Eggie in, laid down in what looked like a crisscross pattern, like the green tiles in her kitchen at home.

It would have been hard to see them the night before, but now, in the daylight, it looked like someone had laid down a carpet of green leading from the nest into the trees.

Ripley stepped carefully over and picked up one of the leaves. Underneath was a thin, razor-like slice in the dirt and a set of footprints, with the toes pointing toward the nest.

"Hey, BARNEY! LOOK!"

Barney jogged over, clutching their book to their chest. "What is it?"

Ripley pulled back the leaves. "Tracks! Different tracks!"

"Hmmm." Barney squinted. "That long thin one? It looks like a tire. You think it's our wheelbarrow from yesterday?"

Ripley shook her head. "The wheelbarrow tire is really thick and it has big treads on it so it won't slip. This track doesn't have any nubblies on it."

Ripley looked up at the nest. "What if someone left the nest with Eggie, but they covered their tracks with leaves. They would do it walking backward, like this, right?"

Ripley mimed what she imagined someone doing, stepping backward, putting a leaf down over the tracks, stepping backward again.

"That would be a pretty great way to cover your trail," Barney agreed. "Great observing, Rip!"

Ripley shielded her eyes and looked to see how long the trail of leaves was. It looked long.

"We just found this," Ripley said. "And they've had a whole day to get Eggie far away."

"We're going to need to move quickly," Barney agreed. "If only we had some form of transport."

Just then, there was a snuffling sound. Like a big soft nose.

Followed by an "AHEM."

Ripley and Barney looked up to see their cabinmates balanced on the back of the very large, chestnut-colored moose named Jeremy.

"HEY!" Hes called down.

Jeremy snorted again.

April, Jo, and Wren waved. "HEY!"

Hes smiled. "Need a ride?"

CHAPTER 18

It was late morning when Rosie passed under the sign outside Miss Qiunzella Thiskwin Penniquiqul Thistle Crumpet's Camp for Hardcore Lady-Types, uniquely frustrated. Which is to say, frustrated was not a Rosie thing to be. Generally, Rosie was unruffled. Cool, like a cucumber that's just come out of the crisper.

But a night of wandering through the trees following a trail that went cold will ruffle the best of us.

Rosie needed to nettle up and regroup.

"You should get some shut-eye," Rosie called back, "if that's something you still do. I'm going out again in an hour."

Bearwoman, who never really slept aside from a scheduled three months of hibernation, was downright cranky.

"We're stopping?" she grumped. "Just because a trail goes cold, you give up?"

"What can I say? I'm *only* human. I need supplies. Food. Water," Rosie said, not looking back. "And then I'll go back out."

"Harrumph," Bearwoman said. Shifting shape, she disappeared back into the woods. "Only human. Very funny."

Jen, meanwhile, was making her way back to her cabin after her morning counselors meeting. She was not expecting a visit from Annabella Panache, who today had opted for a more casual black leotard and silver sweatshirt and was stretching on the steps of Roanoke.

Spotting Annabella, Jen's stomach flipped in that notfun EEK kind of way.

Annabella beamed warmly, holding up her arms and then bowing down to touch her toes.

"GREETINGS," Annabella boomed, her face by her knees. "Is it Jennifer? Yes? I'm never sure."

Jen froze, her face plastered in a terrifying grimace as she gave Annabella a stiff, nervous wave. It looked like she was trying to very quickly wash a very small window with her left hand while smiling.

"Yes." Panache smiled, standing upright, her face flushed. "I was hoping you could assist me in locating a few of your scouts. Some rogue thespians, if you will."

Jen blinked, now sweating profusely. "Oh," she said, because it was the smallest thing she could think of to say, the thing that meant opening her mouth for the shortest period of time.

A thing, like a bubble, was jumping around inside of her, struggling to get out.

Indeed, Jen's face was turning purple. Miss Panache stared, fascinated.

"The workshop of course is going fabulously," Panache said. "Yes. Your scouts, all of them, have been incredibly spirited if sometimes hesitant, yes? To . . . EMBRACE? Still, they were doing very well and then some of them just . . . POOF!"

Panache threw her hands up as though releasing a cloud of glitter. POOF!

"Specifically," she added, "this afternoon, several scouts, it appears, have exited stage left. Including April, Jo, and Ripley."

Now Jen was trying to talk without actually breathing. "Really?" she squeaked.

"Yes. If you could assist in locating them, it would be most appreciated," Annabella said, curtsying. Then she snapped her fingers. "OH YES. I meant to add, I'm sorry we couldn't convince you to join us in our THE-AH-TRICAL pursuit. Maybe get up onstage?"

"SNRK!" Jen's face spasm-ed. "ST-ST-STAGE?" she gulped. "ME ONSTAGE?"

"My dear," Annabella tut-tutted, "you look unwell. Yes? Whatever is the matter?"

Jen couldn't hold it in any longer. A laugh the size of a freight train stormed out of her, "HAHAHAHAHAHA-HAHAHAHAHAHAHAHAHAHAHAHAHAHAHA-HAHAHAHAHAHAHAHAHHAHAAAAAA!"

"Miss Jennifer," Miss Panache gasped. "A most fabulous explosion of emotion? Yes! We can work with this!"

"HAHAHAH!" Jen fell backward, her back twisting and her arms rigid. "STAGE FRIGHT! TERRI-HAHAHAHA-BLE STAGE FRIGHT! MAKES ME LAAHAHAHAAUGH!"

"Hmmmm." Annabella tipped her head. "I don't believe in Stage Fright. I believe in Stage POSSIBILITY! You need to channel this, Miss Jennifer. I sense great potential. Yes!"

Jen fell back in another spasm, her body shaking with earthquakes of hysterical laughter. "HAHAHAHA! NO! HAHAHA. Sorry. HAHAHA. Nope. Excuse me. HAHA-HAHAAA. CAAAHAHAHN'T BREHEEHEETH!"

And with that, Jen twisted in the opposite direction and bolted away from the cabin, both to escape the idea of ever going onstage and to find her scouts.

Meanwhile, Rosie swung by the stables, where she found a note from Hes letting her know that Jeremy had been "borrowed."

"Interesting," Rosie said, thinking maybe now she wouldn't have time to get her nettle tea.

She was right.

CHAPTER 19

Let us take a moment, since we have one, to revel in the joy that is traveling by moose, a very close second to traveling on magically massive kittens named Marigold.

Moose riding has been an honored tradition at Miss Qiunzella Thiskwin Penniquiqul Thistle Crumpet's Camp for Hardcore Lady-Types since Miss Qiunzella Thiskwin Penniquiqul Thistle Crumpet acquired, and trained, her first moose, Roger Masterhead Morningside Marbel Meedoo.

Moo, for short.

Scouts with a passion for moose riding have two badge options, the Get a Moose On badge, for general moose riding, and the Bust a Moose badge, for Moose dressage, which is where moose and rider perform a choreographed routine to a popular song. Only three scouts have ever received the latter of these badges, including Hes and Rosie, mostly because a great number of moose really don't like to dance.

Jeremy was an exceptionally strong, patient, and very large moose who loved to dance and, fortunately, could fit six scouts on his back and still travel at a fairly fast clip.

As Jeremy galloped, Ripley stared at the horizon.

We're coming, Eggie, she thought. We're coming.

The trail of crossed ferns wound through the woods into a field of lavender, where the ferns faded and laid bare the trail Ripley had uncovered earlier that day.

"They stopped covering their tracks," April noted, looking down.

"Maybe they didn't think we would follow this far," Hes offered.

"EGG THIEVES!" April growled. "Think they can just come into our camp and take eggs?! What the Dee Rees is going on here?"

Barney looked at Ripley.

Ripley kept looking ahead. Searching the view for a sign of Eggie. Searching with what felt like her new superpowered observing eyes.

"Hey!" Ripley shouted, pointing at a bunch of trees up ahead.

Jo, leaning over the side of Jeremy with a pair of binoculars, nodded. "I see it! Hold up!"

Hes tugged the reins gently and Jeremy ground to a halt.

Everyone squinted into the distance and strained to listen.

"What is it?" April asked, looking at Rip. "What did you see?"

"Gold," Ripley said. "A little sparkle. In the trees there."

Ripley knew sparkle when she saw it.

"I hear voices," Wren whispered. "About twenty feet away."

Wren, like Mal, had what's called "an ear," which means having an ear that's very sensitive. Or two ears.

"Dismount," Hes whispered, and all six scouts slid off the moose and onto the ground.

"All right, scouts," April and Hes said in unison.

"Ahem," Hes said, taking a small step back. "I'll let you do the 'being the one who says the thing' thing."

"If we're going to Lumber-rescue this properly, and I think we are, we're going to need to take the Maya Lin approach," April said, holding her arms out with the tips of her fingers touching. "Spread out and stay low to the ground 'til we get to the trees and the egg poachers."

"Does everyone have their Mixed Signals badge?" Wren asked. "Because if so, we could stick to hand signals."

Ripley nodded.

Jo gave a thumbs-up.

Hes put her hands on her waist and then nodded three times, which means, in Lumberjane signal speak, "Yes, of course."

Barney knew several different versions of hand signaling, including ASL (which is American Sign Language), but knew this was not the time to go into those details and so just nodded.

April held up her arms. Then dropped them, pointing forward. And then pointed to the ground. Which are the Lumberjane signals for "OKAY, SCOUTS," and "MOVE FORWARD," and "STAY LOW."

By the time they got close to the tree line, faint strains of disco music could be heard wafting through the breeze.

Also, a sort of cement mixer–like shriek. "EU-GENE!"

"EUGENE!"

"EUGENE!"

All six of the Lumberjane rescue party stopped in mid-crawl, hands hovering, muscles frozen. Jo held her breath.

Hes, next to April at the front of the crawling party, tapped her head and pointed.

April nodded and turned behind her.

125

Egg-nappers in sight! she signaled. Move with caution.

Everyone else nodded. Moving slowly and silently to where the shadow of the trees overlapped the grass, they crouched behind a bank of blackberry bushes.

The little green leaves tickled Ripley's chin, but she kept her lips pressed shut.

The Lumberjanes leaned forward and peeped through the branches.

And there they were, the source of all this noise: human creatures dressed entirely in gold.

"EUGENE! I ASKED YOU IF THE GOOSE DOWN WA-TER IS REA-DY?!"

Human creatures in the process, Jo thought, from the smell, of making very bad coffee.

Ripley looked closely, taking in every detail. There were two in the camp. One was tall and curvy and wore a gold hat, a gold jumpsuit, and gold high-top running shoes with big floppy gold laces. This was the one screeching "EUGENE!" like an owl. A really big owl.

The other one, who Ripley figured was EUGENE, was short and skinny, roughly the weight of a Yorkshire terrier, Ripley guessed, or eight chubby hamsters. This one was dressed in a similar gold jumpsuit with a gold safari hat perched on his head, in tall, lace-up gold boots.

Jo flashed to the picture in *The Very Big Book of Curious People*.

Bad food, Jo thought. Tacky outfits. Must be the Order of the Golden Egg!

How curious!

"Golden Goose, Egberta," the man who was most probably Eugene griped. "Get a hold of yourself. I heard you. Stop it with the goose down yelling!"

"If YA HEARD me, YA SHOULD HAVE SAID SO!"

"You are gonna get us caught! What if those crazy army ladies are still following us?"

Army ladies, Ripley thought, meant Rosie and Bearwoman.

The gold woman waved her arms as though batting away a herd of butterflies. "AH, WE LOST THEM MILES

AGO. They don't call me Egberta, master tracker repeller, for nothing, ya know! I even tossed out a few gum wrappers to throw them off our scent! Those STUPID army ladies! Trying to steal our EGG!"

You, Ripley thought, don't even know what we can do. We are LUMBERJANES, and just because we don't have gold pajamas doesn't mean we can't kick—

April touched Ripley's shoulder softly. Where is Eggie? she signaled.

Ripley, wide-eyed, signaled back, Up there!

Up in the trees, Eggie dangled in a hammock of golden ropes.

"What YOU need to be worried about is my goose down COFFEE!"

"Feathers, Egberta, I said stop with your GOOSE DOWN yelling!"

Eugene stamped the ground in his high heel boots. He started pacing in an angry circle, growing increasingly closer to where the scouts were hiding.

Back up, Hes signaled. Before they see us!

Slowly but surely, without even a squeak of noise, the Lumberjanes back-crawled away from the tree line.

Ripley, all the while, looked up at Eggie, sending a psychic message.

I am here, I am Ripley, and I am going to get you out of there.

Okay, April signaled, once they were back at Jeremy, who was contentedly munching on lavender.

"Right," Hes said, quietly. "I don't think they can hear us now. So, I think we can actually talk."

"So that," Jo said, "is the Order of the Golden Egg."

"What's the Order of the Golden Egg?" Ripley asked.

"Them," Jo said, gesturing in the direction of Eugene and Egberta. "They're part of an Order that's obsessed with eggs, and this book I read said they were tacky and had bad taste in food."

"I did sense some beef gum on the breeze," Barney noted.

"Right," Ripley said. "We need a plan."

April looked at Ripley. "Yes! Yes, we do."

"Does anyone HAVE a plan?" Hes wondered.

"They were really loud," Ripley said. "We need something to distract really loud people in tacky clothes."

April snapped her fingers. "Plan!"

"Okay, spill it," Hes said.

April smiled the smile of someone who has a very good plan. "How do we all feel about doing a little ACTING?"

CHAPTER 20

By the time Rosie left the stables, a great wind was gusting through the camp.

Somewhere inside that wind were the beginnings of a sound.

Rosie looked up at the dark shadows in the sky that looked very much like clouds. And frowned.

"ROSIE!" Vanessa bounded around the stables, her hair spikes tossing in the wind. "WHAT IS—"

"GET EVERYONE IN THEIR CABINS!" Rosie shouted. "NOW!"

Quickly and efficiently, counselors gathered their scouts and headed to their cabins.

Rosie started running toward the center of camp, stopping to herd wayward scouts to their cabins.

"Let's go! Let's go! Into your cabins! This is not a drill!"

Mal and Molly were heading back from the music cabin. They were halfway to Roanoke when the wind started stirring and swirling like a cauldron.

"YIKES!" Molly cried, putting her hand on top of Bubbles so he didn't fly off her head and into the woods.

"*TWEEEP!*" Bubbles chirped, clinging to Molly.

"Is it a hurricane?" Mal wondered.

"Grab my hand!" Molly reached back with her free hand.

At the center of camp, the Lumberjane flag flapped wildly, like it was trying to break free and go somewhere less windy. Bearwoman, sitting next to the flag, swayed slightly in the current.

"Bearwoman!" Molly cried.

"B-DUBS!" Mal added, because Mal enjoyed calling Bearwoman "B-dubs" whenever possible. Because it's a cool name, even if it wasn't Bearwoman's actual name, which wasn't even Bearwoman.

"Humph," Bearwoman said, most of her voice caught up in the wind. Bearwoman wondered how long she would let these scrappy scouts call her by something other than her name.

"What's happening?" Molly called into the wind.

"Once again this is none of your business," Bearwoman shouted, adjusting her coat, which was also thrashing in the gale like someone was trying to pull it off her back.

"UH, well, we're kind of standing in it," Mal said. "SO maybe it kind of IS our business this time."

"SCOUTS!" Rosie called as she pushed through the gusts to the flagpole. "You need to go to your cabins!"

"We're going," Molly said. "We just—"

"What's happening?" Mal asked.

"They're coming," Bearwoman growled, adjusting her coke-bottle glasses. "Humph. Just as I predicted."

Mal looked up. "What is that sound?"

"They're *here*," Rosie said, looking up.

The sound. It hit the camp like a hammer. It was a sound of FLIGHT, but thick and heavy like metal, like the kind of metal that holds up buildings or cuts other heavy things in two.

It is curious how the sound of something flying can reflect the nature of the thing that is flying.

Like how mosquitoes, flying in their weaving way, make a sound like a mosquito bite feels.

Or how almost everything humans have created to fly, including Jo's father's many rockets, sounds, accurately, like metal and fuel.

And yet, a flute, the most frustrating instrument of all time, tossed off a cliff, makes almost no noise.

This sound was the sound of wings the size of baseball diamonds, wings as broad as ships, cracking against the air like angry whips. Pierced through with the sound of a blistering shriek:

CERRRRAAAAAARP! CEEEEERRRAAAAAARP!

And there it was, a crest of wings, a sharp beak, eyes as blue as an ocean.

A thick lion's paw touched the earth first, and the ground shook.

"WHAT THE OPRAH WINFREY?" Molly gasped. "What is it—"

Molly's eyes were like saucers. "HOLY G. WILLOW WILSON, it's a GRIFFIN!"

Mal looked at Molly. "A what now?"

CHAPTER 21

A griffin.

A griffin is a massive, very impressive, very dangerous creature that stands, if you can get it to stand still to measure, between fifteen and twenty feet tall. Unlike dragons, which are traditionally reptilian in nature, griffins have the body of a lion, the head of an eagle, a set of thick furry hind paws in the back, and a set of sharp eagle claws in the front.

It would probably be one of the coolest and scariest things you have ever seen, if you had.

But the possibility that you HAVE seen a griffin is so small, even Jo would have trouble calculating it.

It is not even a curious thing to see a griffin. It is an incredibly strange, rare, almost unheard of thing.

It is so unheard of that even Rosie had never stood this close to a griffin before. And Rosie, in all her years as a Lumberjane, had seen a great many things.

So many things it would be impossible and not completely time efficient to list them here.

Of course, as a seasoned and experienced Lumberjane, Rosie knew what to do when encountering something so very unheard of. The thing to do, which relates to the ODD approach actually, is to be very still and very attentive and to try not to do anything upsetting or disturbing.

And so, after watching the front claws of the Griffin hook and rip into the ground, clawing a deep gash as it skidded to a halt only a foot away from where she was standing, Rosie did her best to be very still and very calm.

This griffin was considerably larger than most griffins. Its breathing made the air quake around Rosie. Standing so close to it was like standing next to a raging storm embodied in a creature that seemed created to tear the world to pieces.

The griffin stretched its feathery head toward the sky and opened its beak.

CEEEEERRRAAAAAARP!

Rosie trembled. Just a little. Mostly because the earth was shaking under the griffin's sharp cry.

CEEEEERRRAAAAAARP!

The griffin shook its thick mane of white and gold feathers and lowered its face so it was eye to eye with Rosie, if it is possible to be eye to eye with something so much smaller than you.

Its eyes were the color of the ocean, cold and blue and seemingly endless.

The griffin narrowed its gaze. It swung its tail around, crushing the flagpole like it was a piece of chalk, sending Bearwoman, Mal, and Molly diving for cover.

Rosie called out without turning. "ARE YOU ALRIGHT?"

"YES!" Mal and Molly stood up, shaken but in one piece.

Bearwoman dragged herself up from the ground. "A fine mess," she grumbled.

Rosie breathed a sigh of relief. Taking a deep breath, she lowered her eyes. She held out her hands palms up to show the griffin that she did not have anything in her hands. No weapons.

Again, the griffin raised its beak to the sky.

CEEEEERRRAAAAAARP!

The griffin lifted its claws and brought them crashing down to the earth not an inch away from Rosie's feet.

"We—" Rosie finally spoke, struggling to keep her balance in the gust of the griffin's mighty *CERARP*. "I assure you, we did not take the egg. And we are trying to find it."

The creature sat back and raised its wings up to the sky, unfurling its magnificent feathers.

Bearwoman looked up. "Humph," she said.

The sky was black. The sun was blocked by a flock of winged beasts, descending.

PART
THREE

ACTING OUT!

NOBODY KNOWS I'M A THESPIAN!

The performing arts are an important part of scouting life. The ability to make an audience laugh. Or cry. The ability to tell a story. All these fall under the powers of communication and expression, which are vital to any Lumberjane.

With this badge, scouts will acquire an appreciation for the various forms of theatrical performance, including stage acting, mime, performance art, and improv comedy.

Scouts will also learn to cooperate, combining the talents of actors, technicians, designers, writers, and directors, to produce, stage, and perform their plays. TEAMWORK POWER!

Lumberjanes know that, onstage, a scout has the opportunity to affect hearts and minds, to tell truths, create fantasies, and give insight into the human . . .

CHAPTER 22

Ripley watched nervously from her perch on Jeremy's back while he continued grazing quietly and April's Plan #4520A was laid out in all its glory.

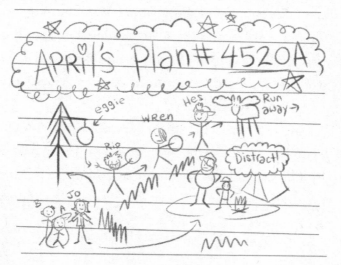

Sometimes, watching these plans unfold felt a little to Ripley like watching a detective show with her brothers and sisters when she was home. Ripley's sister Amy LOVED detective shows and books and movies. She always knew who the bad guy was, no matter what. Sometimes even in the first ten minutes, Amy would sit forward on the couch and point at the screen and say, "Ha! It's that guy, that guy in the hat did it!"

Ripley never saw it. "What?" she'd say, with a mouthful of popcorn.

Amy said the reason Ripley didn't see stuff was because she was a little kid. "You just don't GET IT," she'd sigh.

Ripley would always take another look at the guy with the hat and wonder what it was Amy could see.

Of course, Barney said all you had to do was look closer, and carefuller, and think about what it was you were seeing.

"Okay," April said as the scouts huddled in a circle next to Jeremy. "There's six of us, which means we can split up by twos and take a three-pronged approach: distraction, retrieval, and EGG-scape."

Placing her notebook on the ground, April pointed to the far-right corner. "Here is Eggie, who is being held captive by Eugene and Egberta, who, according to Jo's fortuitous research, we have discovered, are very likely members of the Order of the Golden Egg."

"Do we know there's just the two of them?" Hes asked, pointing at the stick figures April had used to indicate the taller Egberta and the shorter Eugene.

"We've only SEEN two," Ripley pointed out. "But there were lots of footprints by the nest."

"Sure. Two or three, the plan should still work," April said. "SO! Wren and I will pose as lost hikers. We will distract whoever is at the camp, allowing Jo and Barney to release Eggie from the net and pass Eggie off to Ripley."

April looked at Ripley. "You're the smallest, so you can hide in the tall grass, and Barney can do a hidden handoff to you, then take off in the other direction. So it will look like Barney has Eggie, or at least give us a moment of confusion as to WHO has Eggie."

"Like a trick play," Ripley said. "Like football!"

"Exactly!" April said. "And you're small, so it's perfect. You can hide in the grass easy-peasy."

April squeezed Ripley's foot. "Then you'll run with Ripley-like grace and speed to Hes, who will be waiting just beyond the pass with Jeremy."

Ripley smiled. "Bet your Gabby Douglas I will!"

"Hopefully they won't see the handoff and you'll have a clear path." April was closing up her notebook when Hes raised her hand.

"Yes, Hes?" April said.

"Where are you going?" Hes asked, looking at April's plan. "You know? Like, what's your destination?"

"Oh yeah." Wren looked at April. "That's a good question."

"What?" April frowned and pointed at the plan. "We're going here."

"No. I mean, where are the tourists going?" Hes asked. "You know, because they're asking for directions . . ."

"Annabella Panache would say you need INTEN-TION," Wren said, holding her fingers stiffly with great panache.

"YES," Jo concurred.

"Okay." April looked at her notebook. "The tourists will ask for directions to a waterfall. Tourists like waterfalls."

Jo considered. "If Eugene and Egberta don't know where the waterfall is, and they can't help, what else are you going to say?"

"Another thing we could do"—Hes scratched her chin—"is a one-on-one defense, but since we don't know if there's a third player or not on their team . . ."

"I think April's idea is a good idea," Wren said quietly. "It's just like the Goldi-Scout thing. We just need a better story. A better MOTIVATION."

"Yes," Jo noted.

148

THE GOOD EGG

Everyone was quiet, thinking in their individual ways, tapping on lips and squeezing eyes tight.

Ripley started to sing, because that's how Ripleys think.

I met an Eggie
Tucked in a nest
That Eggie was gold
That Eggie was the best
Someone who thinks they love Eggie
More than me
Put poor little Eggie
Up in a tree
Those egg lovers
Aren't lovers
But stealers
If you love Eggie
Don't put Eggie in a tree
I love Eggie
I let Eggie be

"I love your little songs," Barney said, looking at Ripley.

"Thanks," Ripley said, suddenly pink-cheeked. Because sometimes when you sing little songs you're not sure someone is listening. Because small songs are such a quiet thing.

"I wish I had a plan instead of a song," Ripley said softly.

Barney cocked their head to the side, thinking. "Maybe you have both," they said. "I mean, you talked about loving eggs. Maybe that's something we could talk to the Golden Egg people about, since they do seem to really like eggs."

"Holy Janelle Monáe, you're right! We should be, like, egg aficionados," April said, her eyes sparkling. "Egg collectors! OH! Now that is an eggceptional idea!"

"You know who knows a lot about eggs?" Ripley said. "BARNEY."

Barney smiled. "I do. Sort of. I mean, yes, I know a lot about eggs."

"You should go with April," Wren said, chucking Barney in the shoulder. "You'd be awesome."

"You think?" Barney looked down at their hands.

"I think." Ripley nodded.

"BRAVO!" April looked at Barney, sizing up their outfit. "I think we just need a quick costume change."

CHAPTER 23

As part of the camp-wide cabin lockdown, most of the scouts in Miss Qiunzella Thiskwin Penniquiqul Thistle Crumpet's Camp for Hardcore Lady-Types spent the afternoon in a spontaneous in-cabin, camp-wide game of Oligopoly, a game where scouts compete to create an open market in which several small businesses can thrive and compete to benefit the community.

It is a very long game, because it takes a long time and hard work to make a community.

Unfortunately, Mal and Molly were the only members of Roanoke who were not part of the Egg Rescue party, so they were left feeling a little unhelpful and unable to really affect the multiple markets with their tiny game.

"So, Rosie said the griffins are here for an egg," Mal said, peering out the window.

"Maybe it's Ripley's egg," Molly said, also peering.

"It's probably the griffin's egg," Mal noted, with a small smile. "Since Ripleys don't lay eggs."

"Right." Molly sat back on her bunk. "Not Ripley's egg. What did she call it, Eggie? Geez. Whenever I think about other people losing stuff it makes my stomach hurt."

"Aw." Mal put her hand on Molly's hand. "Look. There's no way that's not where April and Jo and Ripley are now. And I bet they're going to get that egg back."

"I hope," Molly said. "I wish we were there helping them."

"Yeah," Mal sighed. "Me too."

"Also," Molly said, in a small voice, "I'm nervous about singing."

"Do you want to practice?" Mal offered. "I mean, since we seem to have some extra time on our hands?"

Outside there were a lot of sounds that sounded very birdlike. Briefly, there had been some pecking on the roof. But mostly there was the grating thwack of wings against the walls and roof of the cabin.

And then, a very human and firm knock on the door.

"Scouts?" Annabella called. "It's Rosie and Annabella. Yes?"

"Yes. Come in," Molly called out.

Annabella was wearing a shirt that looked like a red felt box and a pair of yellow leggings. Rosie was a little bit covered in puffy gold feathers.

"Scouts," Rosie said, crossing the floor, "as you know, we have a bit of a situation in camp today."

Mal and Molly sat down on Mal's bunk.

Mal wondered if maybe April, Jo, and Ripley were in trouble.

"This is about Ripley and the egg," Molly said. "Right?"

Rosie removed her glasses and began rubbing them on her shirt. "It is. Do you know where they went?"

Mal and Molly shook their heads in unison.

Rosie readjusted her glasses with a short nod.

"Girls," Rosie said, "there are serious things afoot, and I'm going to have to ask you for some help."

"Anything," Mal and Molly said in unison.

Rosie adjusted her glasses, "I heard there was a musical in preparation."

Mal nodded.

"I'm hoping you'd be willing to stage a performance for us. For a very specific audience, of griffins."

"Uh." Mal looked at Molly and shrugged. "Sure. I mean, if you think it will help."

"I'm hoping it will be enough to keep them engaged,"

Rosie explained. "Really the last thing we want is a rogue gorgeous (official term) of griffins wandering through camp, running amok."

"Is that something they do?" Molly, who was keenly interested in mythology and the practices of creatures like griffins, asked.

"It's something I hope they won't do," Rosie said. "What I'm hoping is, you can keep them distracted while I see about the egg in question."

"Of course. YES!" Annabella Panache chimed in, her voice powerful and resonant. "MUSIC! SOOOTHES the ANGRY BEAST!"

"In this case," Rosie said, "yes."

"What about the opera?" Molly asked.

Rosie shook her head. "Can't risk it. With griffins, we need something a little less esoteric."

"I think more people enjoy opera than you think," Panache sniffed. "But perhaps that is a debate for another time."

Just then, Jen peeked into the cabin and, spotting Annabella, began to giggle nervously. "Hee hee hee. What's ha-ha-haappening?"

"Team the Scout and the Beast is on deck," Annabella announced, rising dramatically. "To the stage!"

CHAPTER 24

The scene was set. Stage left, April and Barney were poised in the bushes on the west side of the trees. Jo and Wren were crouched in the bushes stage right. Hes was on Jeremy a few yards away, backstage. Ripley hid in the tall grass and lavender, her eyes just peeking out so she could see.

Unaware that they were in for a show, Eugene and Egberta were just about to brew their second cup of horrible coffee and dig into a disgusting slice of turkey toffee coffee cake.

"Okay, ready?" April asked, under her breath.

"Ready." Barney nodded crisply.

"Remember, no small parts . . ." April exhaled, as they walked toward the Order's camp.

"Good luck," Ripley whispered from her hiding spot as she watched the tiny dots that were Barney and April make their entrance. For extra good measure, she crossed her fingers.

"EGBERTA, EUGENE! DARLINGS!" April boomed. Her hair was in a high bun, and she wore Hes's sunglasses and Wren's sweater, which was wrapped around her neck three times. "WE ARE HERE! WE ARE HERE! WE ARE HERE! YES!"

Eugene, who was about to pour the coffee, and Egberta, who was just about to complain that Eugene was taking his sweet goose down time, both stiffened, then jumped up in a frazzled twist of gold bodysuited bodies.

"WHO THE FEATHERS ARE YOU!?" Egberta screeched, waggling her finger at April.

"Goose down, Egberta, stop SCREAMING!" Eugene grouched.

Then, turning to Barney and April, he griped, "Yeah. Who are you?"

Barney was wearing April's white hair tie around their neck twisted like an ascot, also Wren's sunglasses, and Jo's coat, which, on their small frame, looked like a sort of stylish overcoat.

They sniffed and puckered their lips in a dissatisfied pout. "*Obviously*, we are representatives from the Omaha Order of the Golden Egg. We called ahead. What's the problem?"

"We're here to see your fabulous OVA," April cooed, pushing past Eugene. "We were told it was an A-grade specimen. We were told a shell to die for. We were told MUST SEE. We were told GET THERE, BE THERE, ALL THAT."

"That's what we were *told*." Barney rolled their eyes. "I hardly believe it. Seeing as who is HOLDING the specimen in question."

Barney glanced around like they wanted to avoid getting any of the camp on them.

"I mean," they sniffed again, "look at you."

Then Barney threw a look of such powerful disdain, if you bottled it you could destroy a galaxy.

April had to bite her lip to stop herself from smiling. Barney was AMAZING!

"WHAT DOES THAT MEAN?!" Egberta screeched, stamping her foot. "LOOK AT US?"

"It means"—Barney twitched their lips like they smelled a small fart—"*this* branch of the Order has a less than reputable reputation and I can see why."

"WHAT?! WE DO NOT!" Egberta fumed, stamping her foot. "Also, there IS NO Omaha chapter."

"Mmmm, right. Right. Sure. OF COURSE you don't know that there's an Omaha Order." Barney yawned. "Makes me wonder if you're even *legitimate* members, if I'm honest."

"Goose down it. Do you think"—April slapped her hands on her cheeks, in extreme horror—"that these folks are not legit Orders?"

Barney threw their hands up in the air, dramatically. "What can I say? The proof is in the custard!"

"OH, we are members of the Order right and proper, goose down it," Eugene fumed, hoisting up his gold body-suit. "And we can prove it."

"Oh, can you?" Barney yawned. "Really? Wow. Then I suppose you can easily name for me the six largest egg-laying species in order from largest to smallest?"

"SURE, he can!" Egberta walked over to Eugene and punched him sharply on the shoulder. "DO IT, EUGENE!"

"Well, then," Barney said, "let's HEAR it!"

That was the signal to Jo and Wren that both Egberta's and Eugene's backs were turned. Eugene racked his brain.

In a bump of barberry bushes, Wren looked at Jo, who gave the thumbs-up, then pointed toward the tree.

"Let's go," Jo whispered.

CHAPTER 25

Back at camp, another stage was set for a plot about to unfold.

The stage, in this case, was the small platform in front of the now-in-splinters Lumberjane flagpole. Rosie had hung up a red curtain behind the stage. Annabella hastily whipped up a small sign that read: THE SCOUT AND THE BEAST: A MUSICAL. BY MAL, MOLLY, MALKA, MAGGIE MAY, AND MARY.

The camp was eerily empty of scouts, who were still tucked in their cabins working on their board games. This was not a show for Lumberjanes but for the crowd, a gorgeous of not-yet-fully-on-board-with-this griffins scattered throughout the camp, perched on rooftops, on watch and watching with actual hawk eyes.

"Okay," Molly said, fingers trembling as the troupe hunched behind the curtain. "There's no business like show business. Right?"

"This is really weird," Malka said, twirling her drumsticks, her hair plaited into tight braids. "But okay."

"What do you say before a show?" Maggie May wondered nervously. "I know you're not supposed to say, 'good luck.'"

"Yeah," Mary said, wide-eyed, twirling her tuba mouthpiece between her fingers. "What do we say?"

"We say, 'Break a leg,'" Mal said with a grin. "Come on, guys. We have a captive audience of furry-feathered patrons. My mom once performed for a hall of angry seniors with broken hearing aids and the show started right after they ran out of pudding. THIS is no problem. We can do this! On three? One. Two. Three."

"Break a leg!" everyone whisper-cheered in unison.

Annabella Panache took the stage first, having changed into a pair of silver pants and a top made out of what looked like pink baseball gloves. Waltzing into the spotlight, she tapped the microphone at center stage.

"Honored guests, good griffins! YES! Marvelous! And now, in the grand and eclectic tradition of the Lumberjanes stage, I present to you a premiere performance of a brand-new musical, for your viewing and listening pleasure."

Act 1.

Molly and Mal walked through the curtain. Mal carried her guitar and Molly her accordion.

Rosie, crouched on the edge of camp, waited and watched.

"Ahem," Mal said, stepping up to the microphone.

A spark of static reverberated through the sound system, ruffling feathers all around.

CEERRRAAAARP!

CEERRRAAAARP!

CEERRRAAAARP!

The stage, no matter the size of the audience, can be a surreal place. A separate world, with its own light and atmosphere. It feels important and intimidating to be onstage, to have yourself be suddenly so heard, so loud, especially if you aren't used to that.

Molly looked at Mal. Her feet suddenly felt very far from her head. "I'm scared," she mouthed.

Mal smiled. "We're going to be great," she mouthed back, bringing her fingers down against the strings of her guitar in the opening chords to the opening song of the musical.

Molly took a deep breath.

How do you know you can do something? Whether it's singing onstage, or rescuing someone, or climbing a big mountain, or eating the most ice cream anyone has ever eaten, the answer is always the same.

You take a deep breath . . . and try.

Molly pressed the opening chords as Mal began to strum.

Then they both leaned toward the microphone and started singing.

> *You're so furry*
> *Silly creature*
> *Hard to say*
> *What's your best feature*

From the side of the stage, Jen watched with all the pride a person could possibly have crammed in her heart as her two scouts sang together onstage. Jen kept her hand over her mouth in case, being that close to a stage, her nervous laugh fell out. It had always seemed an amazing thing to Jen, what other people could do on a stage, stuff like singing and dancing. Just the thought made her tremble.

It is not a convenient thing when the things that make you scared make you laugh. Especially when it is a thing that, deep inside your heart, you kind of love.

The griffins stirred. As the sweet notes of Mal and Molly's song swept into the air and wafted into the camp, the griffins clucked. Stepping down from their perches, they drew closer—like moths to a flame, or griffins to a song, as the saying also goes—and clustered in front of the stage.

Because while it is true that griffins do not, DO NOT, generally, like humans, it's also true that they love music.

Especially musical theater.

> *Don't need to see past*
> *Scales and fur*
> *To make this love last*

Molly closed her eyes.

> *I just need to seeeee you as you aaaarrrre*

(Once again, songs do not have to rhyme.)

Rosie was hoping this would be just enough distraction, just enough time for her to find Ripley and the rest of the scouts, help retrieve the egg, and get back to camp.

"Keep up the good work, scouts," she whispered, slipping off through the trees, unseen, or so she thought.

CHAPTER 26

It is unfortunate that there was no one around to film Barney's performance as the unimpressed member of the Omaha Order of the Golden Egg, because it was pretty spectacular.

A close second to Abigail Albatross Assander's turn as the star of Jane Wagner's *The Search for Signs of Intelligent Life in the Universe*, which played at Miss Qiunzella Thiskwin Penniquiqul Thistle Crumpet's Camp for Hardcore Lady-Types several years before Barney arrived.

As April did her best to conceal her glee, Barney kept Order egg-nappers Eugene and Egberta running in circles with endless egg trivia. All the while, Jo, up in the tree, sawed through the golden ropes in Eggie's sling with her handy multi-tool.

When the last rope was split, holding her breath, Jo pulled Eggie through the hole in the netting and lowered it into Wren's waiting hands.

"We really are going to have to call the Order and withdraw your credentials if you all can't get this one," Barney scoffed, tugging on their scarf.

"What kind of EGGsample are you setting for your fellow members?" April groaned.

"It's the EMU," Eugene said, tugging on his gold hat. "I know it is!"

"It's really not," Barney chuckled. "Goose down, are you serious?"

"How UN-EGG-ducated!" April sniffed.

"EUGENE!" Egberta screeched, tearing at her hair. "What is wrong with you?"

"Goose down it, why don't you answer some of these, then?" Eugene griped, slamming his safari hat down farther on his head.

Meanwhile, taking quick and quiet careful steps, Wren sped-walked the egg to Ripley.

From her hiding spot, Ripley watched Wren approach. Her palms were sweating, waiting for the moment her arms were wrapped around Eggie.

Meanwhile, as quietly as she could, Wren huffed and hustled through the grass. Sweat was running down the sides of her face; her knees felt like rubber.

Quiet and quick, Wren thought to herself. Quiet and quick.

Also, she thought, Holy Clara Hughes this egg is HEAVY.

Wren's arms ached keeping their grip. Holding Eggie and walking fast made it hard to concentrate on where she was going and on the ground beneath her and suddenly . . .

Wren's stepped down, smack in the center of a large stick lying in the grass, snapping it in two.

Crack!

Wren froze.

Everyone looked up at once. April and Barney. Jo peered down from the tree.

Ripley stayed crouched, her heart banging like a gong.

"EGG!" Egberta screeched, waving her hands over her head. "OUR BEEEEAUTIFUL EEEEEGGGGG! EDGAR! EDGAR! EEEEEGGGG!"

Edgar? April thought.

Who's Edgar? Barney wondered.

The third member of the Order, Jo thought, is . . .

Edgar.

And just then, Ripley thought of the tracks they had followed from the nest into the woods.

A narrow tire track.

Which Barney had thought was a wheelbarrow.

But was not.

ZOOOOOOOOM!

Edgar zipped out from the trees, astride a glittering gold unicycle.

In true Golden Order style, he looked like he'd been dipped in gold. He was six feet tall—on the unicycle he was eight feet—with a thick gold moustache and big bushy gold beard that swallowed up the bottom of his face. He was wearing a full gold pantsuit, with a long train of gold fringe that fluttered in the breeze. On top of his head was a very small (one might say, two sizes too small) gold top hat with a tiny gold pom-pom perched on the top, like a tiny canary.

"GET 'ER, EDGAR!" Egberta screeched.

A unicycle, Jo thought. So that's what that track was.

Wren gasped.

"EDGAR! GET THE EGG THIEF!" Egberta screamed, clearly unaware that she was also an egg thief.

Eugene hopped up and down and pointed. "She's over there! THE GOOSE DOWN EGG THIEF with the PUR-PLE HAIR!"

Wren swallowed hard, and bolted.

Ripley pressed her fingers into the ground and watched Wren's feet approaching. When she got close, Wren crouched slightly, dipping just enough to pass Eggie into Ripley's hands before standing up straight and running off to the left, her back to the Order as she broke into a sprint.

April crossed her fingers. Did it work? It looked like Wren, now running northward, still had Eggie in her arms.

Ripley paused a second, squeezed Eggie tight, then stood up and started running.

Egberta, who had what's called "a good eye," which meant she had great eyesight (not great taste), spotted Ripley immediately.

"THERE'S TWO OF THEM!" Egberta screamed, jogging up and down, waving her arms in the air. "Eugene, follow purple hair! EDGAR, GET THE LITTLE ONE!"

"Oh no," Barney moaned.

Ripley looked back just long enough to see the crazed face of the wheeling dervish that was apparently Edgar heading right for her.

"EDGAR, GET THE LITTLE ONE!"

"RIPLEY!" April screamed. "RUUUUUUUUUN!"

CHAPTER 27

A piece of cake" is a phrase people use when describing something that is relatively easy to do.

For a Lumberjane, the Piece of Cake is an event that takes place near the end of the summer, when scouts are tasked with the challenge of carrying three bowling balls in a basket while running on a complex obstacle course made mostly out of frosting, Victorian sponge, and wood.

And so there is, actually, a strong tradition in the Lumberjane world of carrying heavy things across long distances with many obstacles in the way.

Running with a giant egg across a field is also not a piece of cake.

For the first time in her life, Ripley thought maybe her lungs would burst.

As she huffed and puffed and strained to keep her grip on Eggie, she could hear the whizzing of Edgar on his unicycle behind her and his cackling voice calling out, "I'll get you, goose down egg thief!"

Farther behind her, Ripley could hear the shouts of her cabinmates, now dashing to catch up.

Jo and April were in the lead, but Ripley was so far ahead it would be impossible for them to be of any help in the run for her life that Ripley now had in front of her.

Ripley tried to remember where it was she was supposed to turn. Because April's plan did involve a turn. She wanted to close her eyes and picture the map April had drawn in her notebook, but she was afraid of what she would bump into if she did.

Her hands were getting hot. Eggie was hot. That had not been factored into the plan.

First her palms, then her fingertips started to sweat, and slip. Eggie sank farther and farther to the edge of her grip. Ripley pressed her fingers into Eggie, feeling the bumps of Eggie's shell.

She could hear Edgar panting, hear his unicycle's whirring wheel. He was gaining on her.

Ripley tried to wrap her arms tighter around Eggie.

She took a shallow breath.

And squeezed.

And just then.

Eggie. Slipped.

It was only for a second. Eggie dropped through the ring of her arms, and Ripley watched in horror as Eggie hit the ground.

And then . . .

. . . sprang back up.

As she caught Eggie in her arms, Ripley's mouth dropped open.

Did that just happen?

Did Eggie just . . . bounce?

And for just that second, Ripley stared at Eggie, still running so fast she missed the very turn she'd been trying not to miss. A turn that was the difference between running to Hes and Jeremy and running up a hill, a steep hill, along a road that was about to end . . . abruptly.

"Where is she going?" April cried as she watched Ripley veer to the right, toward the path that led up the side of the mountain on the edge of the forest.

"The wrong way," Jo said.

"YES!" April groaned. "I mean . . . NO!"

Edgar the unicycler grinned a gold, toothy, Order of the Golden Egg grin as he leaned forward and closed in on "the little one."

CHAPTER 28

Back at camp, the griffins—who had been enjoying the musical theater stylings of Mal, Molly, Malka, Maggie May, and Mary, including a very moving scene in which the five scouts gave the Lumberjanes oath an upbeat musical adaptation—were getting restless.

Which is to say that griffins, who enjoy music and musical theater, are also very picky. And finicky. And, well, they like what they like.

And this says NOTHING about the quality of The Scout and the Beast. Truly it does not, but the griffins were rapidly losing interest in this five-piece performance.

The cries of "CERRAARP! CERRRAAARP!" which had started low, like a rumble, were getting louder, with a hint of what Mal thought sounded like frustration.

Annabella Panache murmured encouragingly at the performers from the side of the stage, but at some point, you have to wonder, as Molly did, when a person should take a hint from their audience.

It should be noted that the griffins' behavior was *incredibly impolite* and not in any way acceptable behavior at a theatrical performance. Even if you're watching a show you don't particularly enjoy, you don't make a fuss. You don't flap your wings and you don't interrupt the singing with growls and CERARPs. This is also why griffins perform so few musicals for other griffins.

Because of stuff like this.

CERRRAARP! CEEEEERRRAAAAAARP!

The griffins' fluttering and squawking in front of the stage was getting louder.

Jen watched the ruckus building from her perch stage right.

Jen had seen Rosie slip off into the forest with that very determined Rosie-like look, a look not unlike the look April had when she had a plan. Which meant Rosie was off trying to help April and Jo and Ripley. Which meant Rosie would probably not want the griffins to notice she was gone.

And if the griffins continued to rumble, Jen thought, and lost complete interest in the performers onstage, then maybe that would happen.

That or something considerably worse.

Someone had to do something.

And that someone, right at that moment, was someone who would rather do pretty much anything other than get onstage.

But sometimes there is a part of a person, a small part at first, that is capable of great things.

And so it was—while the rest of the performers were paused between numbers, working up the courage to continue what seemed like it was going to be a very unpopular fifth act—that Jen stepped up onto the wooden stage, walked over to the microphone (which felt oh so far away), and—stifling the laugh tickling every fiber of her being—took it in her hands.

"Okay, um. This is my mom's favorite song," Jen said, her voice wavering and echoing over the sound system.

The griffins, once clucking and rustling, were suddenly still.

Cerrrarp? one clucked. Wary.

Jen closed her eyes, opened her mouth, and sang, "*When I was young . . .*"

"OH! I know this one," Malka hissed from her drum kit, pointing at Mal. "C Major."

CHAPTER 29

Suddenly.

Ripley was alone.

Alone.

And out of options.

Ripley was out of road to run on, literally.

The turn she'd taken to get to where she was had twisted and turned and twisted. As she ran, Ripley searched the horizon in vain for a sight of Hes on her moose, hands out and waiting for Ripley, but Hes never appeared.

And that was when Ripley got that feeling you get when you realize that you are not doing the thing you want to be doing, that you have taken a wrong turn. It is a feeling that would lead one to believe their actual insides are not inside them. That their insides are maybe at the spot where they were supposed to be. That their insides are waiting for them at the end of the left turn they did not take at least a mile back.

It is a complicated feeling.

Ripley had kept running through all that, until she actually couldn't run anymore. Until the ground became the top of a cliff with a very long drop on the other side.

A very very long drop.

The good thing was that the last bits of the path were not easy for unicyclers, so Ripley had gotten ahead of Edgar. But now she was in what is sometimes called a pickle. For some weird reason.

Now, the only way to escape would involve flying.

And Ripleys cannot fly. Nor can eggs.

This is not to say Ripleys cannot do a good many things. Because they can.

Sometimes it's hard to know what those things are, of course. Because there are things people GIVE you to do or SAY you can do. Which makes it hard to think of all the many things you are capable of. Especially when you are all alone, and scared.

"All alone," Ripley said quietly, to the wind.

The wind howled back, unhelpful. It whipped around her and chilled her skin.

Ripley wished there was someone around to tell her what to do. Maybe a Rosie.

Ripley sniffed and squeezed Eggie tight. It was not like squeezing Mr. Sparkles. It was barely a squeeze, really.

A little tear rolled off her cheek and sploshed on Eggie's shell.

"If April were here," Ripley sighed, "she'd know what to do."

Ripley looked down at Eggie, heavy in her arms, and that was when Ripley had a very important thought.

She was not alone.

"Eggie!" she said. "I have Eggie!"

Not only did Ripley have Eggie, Ripley realized, she was *responsible* for Eggie. There was no one to help Eggie but Ripley! Eggie was depending on her to help it. Eggie needed Ripley!

And of the many things Ripleys can do, helping Eggie would have to be one.

Ripley pressed her lips together.

"I won't let you down," she whispered.

There was a gravelly skidding noise, and a panting, and there, through the grasses and leaves, appeared a very tired and very angry gold-wearing unicycler named Edgar, his head bright red and sweaty under his top hat, dragging a unicycle.

"Meddlesome goose down kid," he growled, grudgingly remounting his cycle and resuming the rocking back and forth that unicyclers do. "That's OUR egg! HAND IT OVER! NOW!"

"Ripley!" Another voice in the distance. A familiar voice.

HES!

It was Hes! Waving just a few feet behind Edgar.

And then.

Ripley had an idea.

She didn't even have to sing. It was just there, like a file folder in her mind. There was so much more in Ripley's head for her to use than she'd previously thought possible.

April wasn't the only scout with plans.

Now Ripley had an idea like a little light bulb, shining and bright.

"THIS," Ripley said, squeezing Eggie, "IS NOT YOUR EGG."

Ripley Plan #0001 was about to take effect.

CHAPTER 30

Ripley's plan was the result of several things that Ripley knew, which is the start of all plans.

Ripley knew that Hes was a very good basketball player.

Ripley knew that Ripley was a very good basketball player.

AND.

Ripley had observed that Eggie could bounce.

Ripley locked eyes with Hes. She carefully placed Eggie by her feet. Then she held her arms up in the air and waggled her fingers. Then she blinked her left eye, and then she stuck her tongue out and pretended to sneeze.

Edgar thought that maybe this little girl with an egg was having a fit.

Hes blinked back at Ripley and touched her nose. Which was the Lumberjane signal for "Yes, I know what a bounce pass is, obviously. Let's do this."

Ripley locked eyes with the man on the unicycle. Slowly bending down, she picked up Eggie with both hands.

And then, fast as lightning and with all her might, Ripley tossed Eggie.

Eggie soared over the very surprised unicycler, who would never have thought to THROW an egg.

And then.

Eggie bounced and rebounded, spinning, into Hes's waiting hands.

"HAHA!" Ripley cheered, bouncing up and over Edgar and after Hes.

GAME ON!

Now it's Hes with the egg!

Over to Ripley and back to Hes!

Hes dribbles the egg. A slick underhand pass from Hes to Ripley as Ripley clears the raspberry bushes and rounds the corner!

Some aggressive offensive work by Edgar the mad unicycler, but Rocket Ripley manages a solid misdirection no-look pass to Hardcore Hes, who dribbles the egg down the path!

The unicycler getting aggressive but avoided by Hes with a quick chest pass to Ripley followed by another solid bounce pass back to Hes.

The unicycler zags, Hes dribbles, goes behind the back, passes to Ripley!

The unicycler has lost his balance, he's down, and Ripley is down the path, it's going to go right down to the buzzer, sports fans!

TWEET!

There, in the path, stood Jeremy, nostrils flaring, and on Jeremy's back was a very relieved Rosie.

"Rosie!" Ripley shouted. Raising Eggie up over her head, she gave a final toss, into Rosie's awaiting outstretched arms.

CHAPTER 31

Rosie wasn't the only one waiting beyond the turn. April, Jo, Barney, and Wren, closely tailed by the rest of the non-Omaha members of the Order of the Golden Egg, clamored through the bushes.

"YOU THERE!" Egberta screeched, hiking up her gold pants and popping a piece of beef-flavored gum into her mouth for sustenance. "YOU GIVE US OUR EGG RIGHT NOW OR SO HELP ME DOWN!"

"Yeah," Edgar huffed, rocking back and forth on his single wheel. "You meddling kids!"

"We're not meddling kids," Barney huffed. "We're LUMBERJANES."

"And it's not YOUR Eggie!" Ripley scowled, holding her arms out to guard Jeremy and Eggie. "You STOLE it!"

"We didn't steal it," Eugene fumed. "We FOUND it and we took it. So it's ours."

April shook her head. "I'm 101 percent sure that's not how that works."

"I'm 200 percent sure that's not how it works," Barney added.

"This egg is not a possession," Rosie said. "And as such it cannot belong to you."

"Oh yeah?" Eugene said. "Then why do you get to keep it? Stupid lady."

"YEAH!" Egberta screeched, shaking her fist at Rosie. "You're an egg stealer! STUPID EGG STEALER!"

"You're egg-nappers!" Ripley charged, sticking out her chin. "And don't call Rosie stupid."

"Who are you calling stupid? You don't even know that much about eggs," Barney noted, hands on hips.

The members of the Order of the Golden Egg looked at each other. Like they were sending secret Golden Order signals to each other. Egberta blew a large beef-flavored bubble.

Which is kind of a gross thing to see someone do.

"Assume Olympic Jamaican Women's Bobsled Team defensive position," April said, out of the corner of her lips.

"I don't think I know that one," Wren whispered to Hes.

Rosie, all this time, was preparing to nudge Jeremy into a trot then gallop and get the Mo'ne Davis out of there, when she heard an unexpected but not in any way unwelcome sound.

A flapping sound.

A very loud flapping sound, headed their way.

"Relax, scouts," Rosie whispered, holding Eggie firmly.

Help was on the way.

"Now that we have a moment," Rosie said, knowing she did. "And we have just a moment. First, as Ripley pointed out, it's not nice to call people stupid and shake your fist at people, so don't do that."

"That's true," Jo said.

"Second," Rosie said, "this isn't our egg. We're not keeping it."

Rosie leaned her head back and cried out, loud and clear, "*CERRARP! CERRRARP CERRARP!*"

"What the goose down are you talkin' about, lady?" Edgar stepped forward. "I think you better be handing over that egg now."

CEEERRRRRAAAAARP!

There it was, that sound again, of big wings and parental concern.

Rosie smiled. "We're just holding this egg 'til its dad gets here."

CEEEERRRRRRAAAAAAARP!

"And"—Rosie pointed up—"I believe that's him and the rest of his family now."

CHAPTER 32

Turns out, while the rest of the gorgeous of griffins were staked out at camp, enjoying the musical stylings of Jen, three griffins, including Eggie's dad, had followed Rosie as she snuck away.

Two of these griffins now swooped down and picked up the wriggling and furious members of the soon-to-be-defunct Order of the Golden Egg in their massive claws, carrying them off toward the horizon, to a place far enough away that they were never heard from again.

Eggie's father landed, gently this time, next to Jeremy, and, with his wing, tenderly took Eggie from Rosie's outstretched hands.

A griffin is a pretty amazing thing to behold. Watching

a relieved griffin who has just been reunited with his egg is like watching one of the most powerful things you've ever seen be, like, otter cute.

"What the Odetta," Hes gasped. "It's a GRIFFIN!"

"Holy Amy Heckerling," Barney gasped, "you're right!"

The griffin cradled the egg in his wings, pressing his beak against the shell and making little cooing noises.

"It's not *not* a bird," Barney said, nudging Ripley. "So we were half right!"

A griffin *is* a kind of very big bird. Although they do not enjoy being called big birds, because they are not, because they are also lions.

Hes, in the midst of all the awe and griffin wonder, found a moment to be dazzled over another incredible phenomenon.

"What the Sheryl Denise Swoopes?!" Hes cheered, high-fiving Ripley. "You can play some BALL, girl!"

"You played basketball?" April marveled, chucking Ripley on the shoulder. "That's so cool!"

195

"With Eggie!" Ripley said, pointing at Eggie, now cradled in the griffin's arms.

"That's legitimately awesome," Jo said. "Who knew that griffin eggs could bounce?"

"I observed it," Ripley explained.

"You're so cool," April said, grabbing Ripley in a giant hug. "I'm sorry I ever thought you were just the baby bear."

"I'm Baby Bear and I'm super cool!" Ripley cheered. "I'm BOTH!"

"You guys," Hes gushed, "Ripley pretty much saved the day with her awesome last-minute plan, which pretty much saved Eggie!"

"Because Ripley is the best!" April squeezed Ripley harder.

"Indeed. Well done," Rosie said, pulling gently on Jeremy's reins. "And now it's back to camp!"

And with that, Rosie, who had crossed off one of her many to-dos for the day, disappeared on Jeremy.

Ripley turned for a final final goodbye.

Stepping toward the edge of the griffin's large and imposing paws, she held her hands behind her back and looked up humbly.

"Um, hello," she said. "I don't speak griffin, but, I just wanted to say, I hope Eggie is okay. And I hope all the other eggs are okay."

Cerarp!

The griffin lowered its head, and Eggie, so Ripley could get a closer look.

Crick crick crick!

"Cerarp!" Ripley grinned. "Eggie is hatching!"

April and Hes and Jo and Wren and Barney all leaned in. And so it was this handful of scouts got to see one of the rarest things a person can see.

Rare is not even the word.

Has anyone ever seen anything like this?

If so, it is not in any old books any Lumberjane, including April, had ever read.

The hatching of a baby griffin.

First, one little yellow beak, then a claw, then another claw, then . . . another little yellow beak!

"Hello, Eggie," Ripley whispered. "It's nice to finally meet you!"

"*Cerarp! Cerarp! Cerarp! Cerarp!*"

CHAPTER 33

There have been many great theatrical moments in the history of the Lumberjanes. In addition to *Julia Cesar* and a particularly stunning reinterpretation of Ibsen's work, *No Longer in a Doll's House*, the rickety Lumberjane stage has seen some fabulous stars ascend.

Many said great things of April and Hes's production of *The Good Egg*, which replaced the production of Goldi-Scout and the Three Bears.

The Good Egg is a play about a scout named Bipley, a very brave scout, who finds a golden egg with her friend Parney.

Bipley sings songs, learns how to be more observant, and saves the day.

There is quite a bit of basketball in the play. Which was choreographed by Hes.

Barney played the part of Bipley, and April played the part of Parney.

Jo did the lights, with a complex configuration of different techniques.

And Ripley played the Egg.

Of all the performances presented that day, and all of them were amazing, many scouts thought *The Good Egg*, while not strictly adhering to the original assignment, was a great story, because it is a story about a hero who does not think she has the stuff to be a hero. It is also the story of an egg who thinks she is an egg but she is that and SO MUCH MORE, and she becomes something more than anyone could have ever guessed. Something amazing.

It was a three-hour play, which Bearwoman, who sat in the shadows with a tub of popcorn and watched, thought was at least twenty minutes too long.

Afterward, on her way back to the woods, Bearwoman stumbled upon Rosie, who was finally enjoying a moment of quiet and a well-deserved cup of nettle tea.

"We still need to talk," Bearwoman said.

"I know," Rosie said, with a sip.

"The waters are shifting, calling out," Bearwoman said. "A scout must answer. Who will be that scout? And will she be ready?"

Rosie looked over and spotted Mal and Molly taking their bows on the stage.

"I hope so," Rosie said.

"Humph," Bearwoman said. "If hoping were hay, there'd be no horses."

"That is a strange saying," Rosie said.

Finishing her tea, she made her way back to camp, which was full of the sounds of celebrating, happy scouts, strains of guitar strings, the crackles of campfires, and the twinkling of stars.

SOME LUMBERJANES BADGES!

WILD THINGS
Learn more about the wild, wild world of birds and animals! With this badge, scouts will observe and document creatures in their natural habitats in order to understand how they survive and thrive.

LET YOUR TROMBONE SLIDE
Feeling brassy? Jazzy? Ready to play? Grab your horn and join the band!

"HEAR! HEAR!" GIVE A CHEER
Ready? OKAY! Kick up your heels, cartwheel, and do splits with this badge that's all about making noise for your team of choice. Cheer on your fellow scouts and learn the proper form for a human pyramid. Pom-poms optional.

YODELAHEEEWHOOO WANTS TO KNOW
Tired of shouting from the rooftops? How about a yodel? Learn more about this unique vocal technique practiced worldwide, then find yourself a nice cozy mountaintop and yodel the day away.

WHOOO WHOOOO'S CALLING

Every bird and animal has a distinct voice and song to sing. With this badge, scouts learn to identify and appreciate the calls of the wild.

HATCH YOU LATER

Come out of your shell and egg-spand your horizons with this badge covering egg-erything you egg-er wanted to know about eggs.

AND THE NEST IS HISTORY

Ah, nests! Not just complex woven structures made with natural elements! Whether it's on the ground or in a tree, scouts will learn how to protect the home sweet homes of the many different species of birds that populate the forest.

GET YOUR ACT TOGETHER

Want to cause a scene? ACT NOW! The play IS the thing with this badge in which scouts learn the value of strong dialogue, sets, and direction.

ACTING OUT!

Ready for your close-up? Prepared to take the stage by storm? Scouts will study a variety of techniques and approaches (Streep, Davis, Oh, and Kaling) and learn to express, emote, and slay for stage and screen.

RIGHT ON TRACK

Know your paw from your hoof? Your moose from your deer? Think you have a talon-t for identifying birds and animals from the prints they leave behind? Find out with this badge!

FLOAT YOUR BOAT

Whether it's a canoe for two or a hip ship for a party of five, scouts will learn the basics of ship construction with this building badge for sea lovers.

ANTHROPOLO-ME

Study the world's cultures, and your own, up close and in person with this badge for future scholars of social practices.

GET A MOOSE ON

Grab your saddle and get ready to get a moose on! Also stable maintenance and basic moose care.

BUST A MOOSE

A moose sport that embraces the refined art of dance in which moose and scout glide across the arena in a series of set movements with grace and skill.

MIXED SIGNALS

Get your message out without making a sound. With this badge, scouts learn to send and receive visual signals using hands and flags.

The Lumberjanes head back to camp in
BOOK 4: GHOST CABIN!
Read on for a sample.

LUMBERJANES

GHOST CABIN

THE *NEW YORK TIMES* BESTSELLING AUTHOR
MARIKO TAMAKI
ILLUSTRATED BY BROOKLYN ALLEN

CHAPTER 1

Not every day at Miss Qiunzella Thiskwin Penniquiqul Thistle Crumpet's Camp for Hardcore Lady-Types is amazing.

MOST of them are.

But some of them are less like sunshine and roses and more like a moose burp in a confined, hot moose stall. Times a hundred.

Some of them are less like fresh bagels and more like the stale cookie you find in the bottom of your knapsack when you're really hungry . . .

Crumby.

This particular day at Miss Qiunzella Thiskwin Penniquiqul Thistle Crumpet's Camp started out deceptively well.

It did rain in the morning, but not hard, more of a light mist, like what comes out of a fancy sprinkler system for a fancy lawn, a mist that made the world outside Molly's window look like a rainbow, and she reached down and booped Mal on the nose so she could see it.

"Look," Molly whispered, pointing.

"Holy Jacqueline Woodson!" Mal gasped, sitting up in bed. "Rainbow connection!"

"RAINBOW!" Ripley cheered, bouncing out of the cabin in order to perform her rainbow celebration dance.

"RIPLEY! SHOES!" April called out, chasing after Ripley with sneakers in hand.

For reasons she couldn't explain, Mal couldn't get rid of the ABBA song that had been playing in her head off and on all summer.

ABBA was in no way Mal's favorite band. But some of their songs are just really happy cheesy songs. And Molly made Mal think of happy cheesy things a lot of the time.

Like on this day, for example, Mal was thinking it would be really cool to go pick daisies together. Is there even a badge for that?

"Goodness Grace Paley," Mal groaned to herself as she pulled on her jean jacket and quickly combed her fingers through her hair. "I'm the cheesiest person alive. I'm the cheesiest person alive and . . ."

Mal paused, staring at the spot where normally there would be socks.

"What the Gunta Stölzl?!"

"What's up?" Molly asked from inside her green shirt, which was almost over her head.

"Uh." Mal got down on her knees, searching her drawer with her fingers and coming up empty. "Wow. Seriously? NO SOCKS, like NONE?"

As of recently, socks and thinking about socks had become a very significant part of Mal's life. Which was surprising, because Mal was more into flannel and collector pins (and buttons) than socks.

At first it seemed like Mal had an abundance of socks. Then, recently, a closer examination revealed that what Mal had was actually a lot of left socks.

Then even Mal's right socks—which, really, who can tell the difference?—started disappearing.

Now, disappearing had become officially DISAP-PEARED.

Molly searched the floor, then bent over and picked up a single Mal sock. "Here's one! That's a start? Or, you know, a foot."

Of course, one sock is hardly a victory when you need two.

Mal and Molly hunted and pecked around Roanoke cabin for almost half an hour, while the rest of Roanoke waited in the mist outside.

"We need to do laundry so Mal can borrow OUR socks," April said, tugging on the bow in her hair and channeling their incredibly responsible counselor, Jen.

"Alternately, Mal could switch to sandals," Jo, who was always coming up with solutions, and preferred sensible boots and wool socks, suggested.

"You can't have adventures in *sandals*," April scoffed, because April was always thinking about adventures. "They're OPEN TOE."

Roanoke cabin's friend Barney, who was very much for a stylish sandal but was also very pro-safety, would agree.

"I'm sure plenty of people adventure in sandals," Jo said. "I'm sure people do lots of things in sandals."

A very huge grin spread over April's face. "They could solve a mystery . . . if something was AFOOT!"

Jo paused, soaking in the first pun of the morning. "Right."

Ripley bounced in place, ready for her morning waffles, her blue hair winking in the sun. "You could have a BEACH adventure. Then you could wear flip-flops or no flops and just have TOES."

"Except, Mal plus water equals—" April made an X with her arms.

In the end, Molly lent Mal a pair of her socks, a sparkly yellow-and-white-striped pair with bumble bees on them and MOLLY written clearly on the bottom of the right toe.

"I like you in sparkly socks." Molly grabbed Mal's hand as they made their way to the mess hall, trailing behind the others.

Mal hooked her arm over Molly's shoulder. "I'll try not to lose them."

"It's okay if you do," Molly said. "I'm not super sock oriented or anything."

Mal stepped into the noisy mess hall. "I feel like socks have weirdly become like the mystery of my life! Like, SOCKS, you know?"

April poked her head between the two of them. "I just wanted to say, your socks are the BEE'S KNEESOCKS!"

Molly rolled her eyes.

"The bee's TOES!" Ripley corrected, grabbing the syrup.

Jo watched as Ripley began stacking what would eventually be a tower of twenty pancakes onto her plate.

Mal grabbed a fork. "Looks like it's shaping up to be a record-breaking kind of day."

"I'm gonna put all these in my belly!" Ripley cheered.

And then, miraculously, given her size, which was not much taller than a stack of twenty pancakes, Ripley did just that.

It was one of a few awesome things to happen that day, but it was pretty awesome.

Just as Ripley folded her final forkful into her face, there was the familiar clomp of Rosie's stride to the front of the room.

"Listen up, scouts!" Rosie bellowed. "Myself and Counselor Jenae—"

"Jen," Jen corrected, without missing a beat.

Rosie continued. "—have a big announcement!"

April jumped up from her seat. "WHAT THE REBECCA SUGAR! RIPLEY JUST ATE TWENTY PANCAKES!"

"Fabulous." Rosie pulled out the giant mail sack. "Also. Mail's here."

In an effort to achieve some level of consistency with the mail, Camp Director Rosie had recently turned all the postage-related responsibilities over to SPARKLE FORCE, a troupe of former scouts who ran special ops tactical maneuvers and rhythm and movement classes for active seniors.

As a result, for the moment, the mail was on time.

Rosie pulled out the first letter while Jen held the sack open. "Listen up for your name to be called."

The bag was covered in what looked like pearly white sand, which Rosie didn't explain, and Jen didn't ask about, because sometimes you have to save up your questions for the big things. The bag was also full of packages and, by some strange coincidence, there was a package for every member of Roanoke.

"APRIL!" got a set of puffy unicorn stickers from her favorite aunt and a new set of fountain pens from her dad.

"Finally," April sighed, "I can make my MARK! Get out a little bit of this PENt up creativity."

"We get it," Mal said.

"JO!" got a teeny-tiny screwdriver that looked like it should maybe be for an elf or a faerie but was actually for people who liked to take really tiny things apart, like Jo.

"Hey, it's A MINI DRIVER!" April boomed. "GET IT?!"

"RIPLEY!" got a MASSIVE box of peanut butter and hot pepper cookies, her mom's secret recipe.

"MAL!"

Mal dug greedily into her package. Mal's mom always sent the coolest things. Sometimes she sent cookies from Mal's grandma, which were often covered in cat hair (from her grandma's dozen cats) but pretty good once you got the fuzz off. Today it was sheet music for Mal and Molly's now pretty decent accordion trio, which still didn't have a name, and a box of caramel corn.

"MOLLY!"

Isn't it amazing how a seemingly possibly good day can turn in the same amount of time it takes a cat to scratch, which is not a lot of time?

Amazing is probably the wrong word.

It's actually more of a bummer.

Molly looked at the package Jen had placed in front of her, covered in neat rows of stamps. She bit her lip.

The box was wrapped in thick brown paper and tied with string. It weighed slightly more than a box of rocks.

"What is it?" Mal asked, leaning over to see.

Molly sighed, melting down onto the table. "It's from my mom."

CHAPTER 2

ere are things that are fun to get in a package:

Lollipops

Hiking equipment

Comic books

Letters from home

Pictures of kittens

Stickers

Socks

Brownies/cookies

Also acceptable:

Band-Aids

Your allergy medication

Sunscreen

More clothing labels

Batteries

Insect repellant

Oatmeal packets

These things can always be shipped in generous quantities so they can be shared and bartered as needed.

Clearly Molly's mom was not aware of this basic package protocol.

Mal watched as Molly gingerly pulled on the twine holding the bundle together, twisted with one of her mother's infamously impenetrable knots.

"Is it socks?" Mal asked hopefully.

"I doubt it." Molly peeled back the thick construction paper, her expression pickled into a sour grimace Mal only saw when Molly got word from home.

The package was full of thin blue exercise books, all labeled MOLLY and covered in Post-it notes with detailed instructions like "Complete me first," "Concentrate, Molly," and "Try to focus and not get distracted, as is your habit."

Mal wrinkled her nose. "What is that? Is that a Post-it note? Is that MANY Post-it notes?"

It is well known that IF you are going to send homework to someone at camp, which you should not do, the ratio of homework to candy or something fun should be no greater than 1:12.

That means for every PAGE of homework you send, you should send twelve other really cool things (see list above).

Almost no one JUST sends homework to camp.

Because it's called HOMEwork.

Not CAMPwork.

Or CAMPfun.

But, as Molly's mother's Post-it notes explained, Molly was expected to use at least some of her time at camp to improve her chances of getting better grades at school the following year.

It should not be suggested that Molly was a bad student. Even Jo knew that not especially liking math does not a bad student make.

(Please note that the sending of books to people at camp is highly encouraged. THIS is a book. Books are awesome.)

Mal watched Molly sink into her seat, like someone was slowly releasing all the Molly out of Molly right in front of Mal's very eyes.

Without thinking, Mal snatched the package. She wanted to erase it.

Molly sighed another long, slow sigh. Like she was suddenly the most tired person.

"So, I guess . . ." She scratched her head. "Um, what are we doing now?"

"We . . ." Mal tucked Molly's unwelcome package under her arm. "WE are going to go have a wicked Lumberific day."

"You said it." April nodded. April was always up for Lumberificness.

"My stomach kind of hurts, but yeah," Ripley said, dabbing at the syrup on her face.

"Seems like a good day for it," Jo chimed in.

"Sure." Molly sighed once again. "Okay."

April looked at Jo, who looked at Ripley, who was looking at Molly. Bubbles, Molly's trusty pet raccoon, who also liked to sleep on her head like a hat, climbed down from his perch on Molly's head and pressed his little furry face against her forehead.

"Squirp!" he chirped.

"Thanks, Bubbs," Molly said.

Mal frowned.

No, she thought. NO. A stupid package is not going to ruin Molly's day!

It would be fixed. MAL would fix it.

"Come on," she said, hooking Molly's arm. "I have an idea."

LUMBERJANES
THE GOOD EGG

MARIKO TAMAKI
ILLUSTRATED BY BROOKLYN ALLEN

LUMBERJANES
GHOST CABIN

THE NEW YORK TIMES BESTSELLING AUTHOR
MARIKO TAMAKI
ILLUSTRATED BY BROOKLYN ALLEN

LIKED THIS BOOK?
THEN CHECK OUT THE BACKSTAGERS!

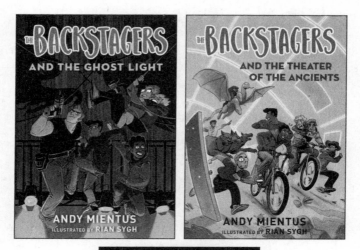

AVAILABLE NOW!

Calling all hardcore lady-types!
See where the adventure began in

The graphic novels that inspired the novels!
Available wherever books are sold

MARIKO TAMAKI

is a writer known for her graphic novel
This One Summer, a Caldecott Honor and
Printz Honor winner, cocreated with
her cousin Jillian Tamaki, among other
notable novels. See her work at
marikotamaki.blogspot.com.

BROOKLYN ALLEN

is a cocreator and the original illustrator
of the Lumberjanes graphic novel series
and a graduate of the Savannah College
of Art and Design. Brooklyn's website is
brooklynaallen.tumblr.com.